Kaya breathed faint.

She weakened, luxuriated in the fantasy that he loved her, that this was a normal situation... that they were lovers waking up to the beauty of becoming parents together.

The fantasy didn't last.

"Leo, I know I didn't have to come here to tell you this face-to-face, but I didn't think it was something I could convey over the phone or worse, by text..."

Kaya watched the way he went very still and before he could start guessing games, unconsciously dodging the obvious, she said quietly, "Leo, I'm pregnant."

Hot Winter Escapes

Sun, snow and sexy seductions...

Whether it's a trip to the Swiss Alps or a rendezvous on a gorgeous Hawaiian beach, warming up in front of the fire or basking in the sizzling sun, these billion-dollar getaways provide the perfect backdrops for even more scorching winter romances and passionately-ever-afters!

Escape to some winter sun in...

Bound by Her Baby Revelation by Cathy Williams

An Heir Made in Hawaii by Emmy Grayson

Claimed by the Crown Prince by Abby Green

One Forbidden Night in Paradise by Louise Fuller

And get cozy in these luxurious snowy hideaways...

A Nine-Month Deal with Her Husband
by Joss Wood

Snowbound with the Irresistible Sicilian
by Maya Blake

Undoing His Innocent Enemy
by Heidi Rice

In Bed with Her Billionaire Bodyguard
by Pippa Roscoe

All available now!

Cathy Williams

BOUND BY HER BABY REVELATION

HARLEQUIN
PRESENTS

ISBN-13: 978-1-335-59214-9

Bound by Her Baby Revelation

Copyright © 2023 by Cathy Williams

For questions and comments about the quality of this book, please contact us at CustomerService@Harlequin.com.

Harlequin Enterprises ULC
22 Adelaide St. West, 41st Floor
Toronto, Ontario M5H 4E3, Canada
www.Harlequin.com

Printed in U.S.A.

Recycling programs for this product may not exist in your area.

Cathy Williams can remember reading Harlequin books as a teenager, and now that she is writing them, she remains an avid fan. For her, there is nothing like creating romantic stories and engaging plots, and each and every book is a new adventure. Cathy lives in London, and her three daughters—Charlotte, Olivia and Emma—have always been, and continue to be, the greatest inspirations in her life.

Books by Cathy Williams

Harlequin Presents

Desert King's Surprise Love-Child
Consequences of Their Wedding Charade
Hired by the Forbidden Italian
Bound by a Nine-Month Confession
A Week with the Forbidden Greek
The Housekeeper's Invitation to Italy
The Italian's Innocent Cinderella
Unveiled as the Italian's Bride

Visit the Author Profile page at Harlequin.com for more titles.

CHAPTER ONE

KAYA QUIETLY LET herself into the house. Frankly, she didn't have the energy to be anything *but* quiet, because she was dead on her feet and brutally cold.

She could feel the February freeze seeping through the layers and pinching her fingers and toes through her boots and gloves. Her cheeks were stinging. She hadn't slept in twenty-four hours and all she wanted to do now was throw herself into her bed and sleep for a hundred years.

The hall light was on. Why was the hall light on? Had she left it on? She'd done a checklist before she'd left Canada for New Zealand two months ago. Would she have written, "remember to switch hall light off"? Unlikely. But Mrs Simpson, who was her nearest neighbour, had keys to the house. Maybe she'd come in to check and forgotten to switch it off.

None of that mattered.

What mattered was sleep.

She dumped the suitcases on the ground along with her coat and shoes, flexed her sore muscles and padded up the stairs.

Kaya knew this house like the back of her hand because this had been her home for the past three years, all thanks to Julie Anne's kindness and generosity. She'd just about managed to make ends meet at university, picking up part-time jobs wherever she could find them to cover her accommodation and her expenses. Then she'd returned back home, clutching her well-earned degree, to find the cost of renting somewhere without much money in the bank and a job yet to materialise beyond her grasp.

Had her mother still been renting their apartment in town, things would have been just fine, but Katherine Hunter had decamped to New Zealand six years ago with her newly acquired husband. Going to her with a begging bowl had been out of the question, the sort of last resort that hadn't even featured on Kaya's radar.

Her mother had finally found her Mr Right, after a lifetime of disappointing relationships with rich guys who'd had no real interest in her, and there was no way Kaya was going to test the marriage by asking for favours. It wasn't as though her mother had any money of her own to throw around and her flamboyant, adorable husband—kind and lovely as he was—simply wouldn't have the means, or probably the inclination, to help out a stepdaughter he barely knew.

So the offer from Julie Anne to lodge with her rent-free had been manna from heaven and Kaya had never, not once, stopped thanking her lucky stars for the older woman's kindly intervention.

Heading upstairs, she paused and took a moment to think about Julie Anne, pushing away the tears pricking the back of her eyes. How could someone so fit, so vibrant, so healthy... so *good*...have died without warning?

Kaya had been working when she'd got the call from the halfway house that Julie Anne had been rushed to hospital—and not the small, local hospital but the one in Vancouver that was over an hour away.

Julie Anne had been talking to Louise, the manager, chatting and laughing, doing the round at the halfway house as she always did on a Friday, when she'd suddenly collapsed. Just like that. Louise had barely been able to talk through her hysteria and tears.

Kaya had rushed to the hospital and had just about made it there to hold her friend's hand and tell her how much she loved her before the life force that had inspired so many over the years had been snuffed out. She had barely taken in the details: an aneurysm…nothing could have been done…a genetic time-bomb waiting to go off… In the end, what had the details mattered when Julie Anne was no longer there, whatever the reason?

She felt as if she'd spent so long crying. There'd been weeks of tears as Julie Anne's death had sunk in, tears for the friend she'd lost—and, as she'd discovered to her confusion and shock, the friend she had not known half as well as she'd thought she did.

So many disclosures and revelations had come in the wake of her untimely death, disclosures she had accepted because there had been no option *but* to accept them. And, anyway, how well did she ever know anyone when she got right down to it? She had resigned herself to the sadness of knowing that Julie Anne had not been the open book she had thought and had focused on all the good she had brought with her instead—focused on the wonderful woman she had been.

In truth, Julie Anne had been her mentor and best friend, despite the age gap. Kaya had known her since she and her mother had moved to this part of the country north of Vancouver and close to Whistler, where her mother had worked. She could barely remember the distant mists of time before that, because she'd been very young, not quite six. She and her parents had lived in Alaska, her father's homeland.

When he had died, they had migrated here, and Julie Anne had become part of both their lives. She had babysat a young Kaya and then, later, taken her under her wing and covered all those times when Katherine Hunter had been out and about with her rich suitor. Katherine had always been more of a pal to Kaya than a mother and never one to curtail her social life to accommodate a child.

Within minutes of decamping to Canada, to this part of the world where she had grown up, Katherine had vigorously contacted all her old connections—not that there had been that many after more than a decade's absence. With single-minded focus, she'd caught up with the town news in record time and concluded that, if help was needed with her young child, then Julie Anne—well known, active in the community and with no ties of her own—would be a very handy babysitter indeed. And so she had been: cheerful, obliging and happy to pick up the slack.

In a lot of ways, their lives had been entwined for so long and in so many ways that she'd been more like a mother to Kaya than Kaya's own mother had been.

Kaya fought back surging memories.

As she quickly and quietly headed to her bedroom on autopilot, she removed layers of clothing. She'd dumped the thick waterproof coat and her fur-lined boots in the hall, and now she wriggled out of the chunky cardigan and slung it over the banister, then the thin, long-sleeved top she wore underneath.

This just left her in a tee-shirt and the baggy, comfy jogging bottoms she had donned for the flight over from New Zealand. Being cooped up in cattle class on a fourteen-hour flight required the sort of clothes that allowed for a lot of body contortions in a confined space, especially when she was as tall as she was.

It was warmer in here than she'd expected. She had returned to freak weather conditions that had dumped inordinate amounts of snow from Alaska down to Florida. The hour and a half that it should have taken the coach from Vancouver had stretched to three, battling blizzard conditions for much of it. But at least she wasn't half-freezing to death in here, and she wasn't going to think too hard about that one.

With thoughts of bed, and forgetting about the shower because that could wait until morning, Kaya pushed open the door, yawning and rubbing her eyes and not bothering to switch on the light. All she wanted to do was fall onto the mattress, pull the duvet over her and close her eyes.

She wasn't expecting anything to be amiss, so it was with delayed reactions that she realised that someone else was in the darkened bedroom...that someone else was sleeping *in her bed*...and that that someone else was a man...

What the hell was a man doing in her house, in her room, in her bed? Flight or fight?

No question. Fight.

Leo hadn't heard the soft opening of the front door or the swift gust of wind that momentarily blew through it but he *had* heard the sound of footsteps stealthily approaching the bedroom along the carpeted corridor that hived off into various rooms, including one that was locked for reasons unbeknown to him.

What the hell...?

Thirty-six hours! He'd been here, in the town that time forgot, for *thirty-six hours* and he was already deeply regretting the journey he'd made.

Hell, he could have wrapped up all the paperwork from the comfortable, warm, luxurious surroundings of his New York offices. Instead, what had he chosen to do? Come here.

Driven by what, exactly? A thirst to discover the joys of small-town living in the heart of British Columbia? A sudden need for vast amounts of space? The scenery—the little he had managed to glimpse—was eye-wateringly majestic, but he was a city guy, someone who thrived in the jungle of streets and skyscrapers, at home where big money was made, and the cut and thrust of deals being done had a heartbeat of its own.

No, he'd come because he'd been curious.

A private jet and the solid four-wheel drive waiting for him at the airstrip had brought him here, and no sooner had he arrived when the weather had decided to make an appearance. The snow had begun and it was obviously here for the long haul. He'd just about managed to make it to the local shops to stock up on food and drink, and since then he'd been holed up here, without Internet connection and plenty of time to rue yielding to the temptation of seeing a past that had been denied to him.

The last thing Leo needed in the early hours of the morning was the tedium of having to dispose of someone who'd broken in in the hope of escaping the snow storm swirling outside.

He'd remained where he was, waiting for developments. The development that opened the door was not one he had expected. He'd figured on a guy, maybe a teenager or a couple of teenagers out and about in the dead of night, doing whatever they shouldn't have been doing in a small town where everyone probably knew everyone else—smoking or drinking and then suddenly realising that, if they didn't find shelter, they stood a good chance of dying of hypothermia. They probably knew that the house had been lying vacant and hadn't thought twice about breaking and entering.

A couple of drunk teenagers? He could have dealt with that. He could deal with anyone, if he was to be honest. A tough upbringing in foster care had served as sterling preparation for pretty much anything. From the minute he'd been able to walk, he had learnt how to handle himself and, the older he had got, the better he had become at it. Nothing scared him. The only scary thing he had ever faced had been the dawning realisation that he had been abandoned as a baby and that nobody would be coming to rescue him—ever. When faced with that, something as hard as granite settled in the soul and nothing, however frightening, could ever compete.

Every muscle in his body was primed for action as he sat up. His senses were on full alert and he was as still as a predator waiting for its prey to make the first move.

The door was pushed open. No lights were on, but still, there was no need for a light for him to realise instantly that his intruder was a woman.

'Who the *hell* are you and what are you doing in this house?'

That from the figure framed in the doorway, giving Leo no time at all to frame his own question, which would have replicated what she had just hurled at him, word for word.

The overhead light was slammed on, and for a couple of seconds he was rendered speechless at the sight of the furious avenging angel glaring at him.

She was tall, at least five ten, slender with very long, dark hair trailing from underneath a woolly hat and she was olive-skinned. And she was exotically and unusually beautiful.

'Well?' she demanded, folding her arms, making sure to stay right where she was within easy reach of backing out of the room and slamming the door shut just in case he tried to reach her.

Smart move, Leo thought, although the last thing he wanted to do was frighten her. His instinct was to push aside the duvet and get out of the bed but he remained where he was so that he didn't spook her.

'I could ask you the same thing,' he threw back at her.

'How did you get into this house?'

'The legitimate way.'

'I know for a fact that that's a lie! I don't know who you are, or what you're doing here, but I want you out!'

Curiouser and curiouser, Leo thought, driven to stare at her because she was so physically compelling to look at and he hated the feeling of being caught on the back foot.

'You would toss a poor guy out in a blizzard?' he asked, blatantly sidestepping the fury on her face.

'Without a second thought!'

'I'm thinking that we need to have a little chat.' He pushed aside the duvet to slide off the bed.

'Don't take another step!'

'Or else what?'

'Or else…'

They stared at one another. Kaya's heart was thudding so hard that she found it hard to breathe.

There was a man in her bed—and not just *any* man. This was the most spectacularly beautiful man she had ever seen in her life. His skin was burnished gold, his hair as dark as hers and his features were so classically perfect that he could have been a lovingly sculpted statue into which life had been breathed.

A spectacularly beautiful *half-naked* man,

and heaven only knew what was happening underneath the duvet. Was he *completely naked*?

Her mouth went dry.

His clothes were strewn on the ground. Glancing quickly at the scattered pile, she got the impression that they weren't off-the-shelf cheap. From where she stood, primed for flight if need be, the coat dumped on the ground looked very much like cashmere.

Gripped with sudden confusion, she remained dithering, her empty threat dangling in the air between them.

'Well?' Leo prompted. 'No, scrap that. I have no idea what's happening here, but I think it's worth a discussion, not least because I have no intention of stepping out into that blizzard and taking my chances because you've decided to point me in that direction.' He flipped back the duvet, stood up and Kaya…stared.

She was tall, taller than a lot of the guys she knew, but this man was considerably taller. He stood well over six feet…and he was all muscle, sinew and six pack.

Black boxers were slung low, revealing a flat stomach and a spiral of dark hair going down to…

She licked her lips and looked away hastily but she was burning up.

She was also at a loss as to what to do. The

man was right—there was no way she could chuck him out into that snow storm. The taxi she'd taken to get here had been fully equipped with all the necessary fittings to deal with severe weather, but even so it had struggled. She hadn't seen any car out the front, so what was he supposed to do—walk until he could no longer fight the weather?

'It's late and I'm tired,' she said tersely. 'You're in my bedroom and I want you to get out of it. I don't care where that takes you.'

'*Your* bedroom?'

'I can't make you leave it, because you're bigger than me and stronger than me, but don't for a minute think you scare me because *you don't*.'

'You think I would *ever*…? No… I can't believe I'm hearing this! And what do you mean by *your* bedroom?'

'I just want to sleep.' Tears of frustration, disbelief, confusion and sheer rage threatened her composure.

Leo shook his head, raked his fingers through his hair and stared at her for a few long, silent seconds.

'Okay,' he conceded slowly. 'I'll decamp and let you have the room, although I have no idea why, considering you've broken into my house. Call me a sucker for a damsel appearing to be in distress.'

Kaya's mouth fell open.

'Broken into *your house*?' But already the wheels were turning in her head as shock and panic slowly began to give way to a creeping sense of dread. No! Surely not…? *It can't be, not yet…*

Leo didn't answer.

'We can discuss this in the morning.' He began reaching for the clothes he had discarded: the tee-shirt on the ground, the jeans slung over the back of the chair and his computer because he might write a few reports even though with no connection he couldn't send them anywhere.

'In the *morning*?'

'I believe you said you just want to sleep.' He vanished into the *en suite* bathroom, leaving her to stew. In his experience, silence could be a man's best friend when it came to getting someone else to talk, and whatever the hell was going on here a talk was needed. He grabbed the towel he had been using and returned to find her barring his exit from the room, the very essence of feminine fury.

'This is where I live and I want to know why you're here!' Kaya shouted at him, but her head began to throb as they stared at one another, and she could detect a creeping hesitancy in her voice. Those piercing dark eyes pinned to her face made her think that he could read every thought in her head.

He'd said he'd entered 'the legitimate way'. All the signs were pointing in one direction, but she didn't want to read those signs, and the destination to which they led was one she had resolved never to visit.

She'd disappeared off to New Zealand to see her mum and stepfather, to escape the cloying misery and sadness she had felt when Julie Anne had died. She hadn't been able to focus, hadn't been able to get past her feeling of drift— she had just needed to *get out*.

Of course, she'd worked remotely from New Zealand, doing the accounts for a range of local and not so local businesses, but aside from that she had just taken time off.

Having spent her youth making sure her mum was all right, supervising her relationships and being the shoulder to cry on, for the first time she had gone to her mother for support. With oceans and continents separating her from her woes, she had allowed herself to forget the reality of what might be happening back in Canada.

It was enough that she had had to deal with the secrets Julie Anne had carried with her so once she'd left Canada she had turned her back on all of that, swept it under the carpet.

'Where have you been?' Leo asked, tiptoeing

around her with the delicacy of a hunter well aware that the beautiful, snarling cheetah might attack at the slightest provocation. 'No, perhaps I should ask you first of all what your name is.'

'Kaya.'

'I'm Leo. I'm happy to continue this conversation in the morning, but with every passing second I'm getting the impression that there is a lot of ground we need to cover.'

'You said you got in through legitimate means...'

'I give you...' He reached into his jeans pocket for a key, which he proceeded to dangle in front of her. There was a tag on it. 'Key to the kingdom.'

'I need to sit down.'

'You look as though you need more than a chair. Why don't we head down to the kitchen and I can give you something stiff to drink?' He held both hands up in a gesture of surrender. 'And I assure you that you have absolutely nothing to fear from me. We can cover some basic ground, because you're not the only one with questions, and then you can have the bedroom, lock the door and go to sleep.'

Kaya nodded, in a daze.

'Are you going to pass out on me?'

'No,' she whispered. 'I'm not the passing out kind.'

'Glad to hear it.'

He stood aside, waiting for her, and she had to control a shiver as she preceded him out of the bedroom and down to the kitchen. She felt like a convict being escorted back to prison, her gaoler behind her making sure she didn't try and pull a fast one. It was colder out here in the hall and she bent to grab the jumper she had discarded earlier and pulled it over her without looking around, without wanting to see the guy walking behind her.

He had a key.

The legitimate way...

Of course, she knew who he was. He wasn't some random stranger she had found sleeping in her bed. He hadn't trudged in from the cold, dumped his cashmere coat on the ground, kicked off his hand-made shoes and fallen asleep in her bedroom.

Because he didn't look like Julie Anne didn't mean that he wasn't connected to her, wasn't related to her. The guy the lawyers had told her would be coming wasn't supposed to be here yet; they had said it would be a long time, not until everything had been sorted out. And the ins and outs of a tricky probate could take up to a year...more than enough time for her to gather herself and find alternative accommodation.

Those lawyers had been very sympathetic.

They had understood the level of her shock when they had called her in to their posh office in the heart of Vancouver and advised her that the house she had been living in, the place she'd called *home*, would be under new ownership.

Julie Anne had left a will and everything would be going to her son.

'Julie Anne doesn't have a son,' Kaya had told them without batting an eyelid. She hadn't had a clue as to what her friend had decided to do with her house and the land, not to mention the halfway house in the middle of town. She had vaguely figured that the halfway house would be kept and the house and land might be sold, with the proceeds going towards the charitable organisation Julie Anne had founded decades ago.

But a son?

She had been frankly incredulous until they had explained, very slowly and very gently, that they had all the documentation to prove his legitimacy. They had explained it to her in three different ways, had brought her innumerable cups of tea and had told her that she could remain where she was, looking after the place, until the legal work was done and every detail sorted. She would have warning to vacate, they had said.

On top of everything else, that single revelation had hit Kaya for six. To know someone and yet not to know them… To discover that there were secrets lurking beneath the surface, secrets never divulged even to her…

She knew that she had escaped more than just her misery when she'd fled to New Zealand. She'd also been running from her confusion and bewilderment at what Julie Anne had held close to herself her entire lifetime. For reasons Kaya respected, of course, but still…

At any rate, she had returned to Canada, ready to pick up the threads, safe in the knowledge that she would be long gone before anyone rocked up to take over the house.

It seemed that fate had had other things in store for her. Thinking about what was happening now made her feel sick, because it raised a host of issues she didn't feel equipped to deal with, not just yet.

She hadn't wanted to meet the son. She'd pushed his existence to the back of her mind, had barely entertained any curiosity about the man. Who was he? What had he been doing for all those years? Had he been a down and out, forced into a life of penury because of circumstances beyond his control? Drifting this way and that before discovering himself to be the lucky recipient of a fortune he hadn't banked on? She'd parked all those questions and focused instead on making sure she wouldn't be around when she got that call from a lawyer telling her that the son would be heading to the house to claim what was rightfully his.

Glancing back at her as he pushed open the kitchen door, Leo noted the wariness on her face and something else—something he couldn't quite put his finger on.

'We're here,' he advised brusquely. 'The snow's falling thicker and harder with every passing second. I think it's fair to say that we're going to have to trust one another, because we're going to be cooped up in this house for a least the next few hours, if not days, and I don't see either of us having much success if we try to make it into town. Or even to the nearest neighbour who lives…where, exactly? I didn't drive past too many houses on the way here.'

Kaya nodded.

What was his plan? Was he really who she thought he was? How could he *not* be? She felt his eyes on her, darkly intrusive and assessing.

Of course he would be curious about her.

More than that, he was right insofar as they were stuck here together in a snow storm and would have to work around one another, however much neither of them might want that. So wouldn't it be wise to keep her counsel? Give herself time to find out what she was dealing with—*who* she was dealing with? Give herself time to adjust to this unwelcome situation?

He didn't look like a down-and-out lucky enough to have landed himself a house and land. There was something smart and sharp about him, something undeniably refined, but she wasn't going to be an idiot and trust first impressions.

She was briefly reminded of the way time and again her mother had fallen for first impressions, for the rich guy, the smooth talk and the easy charm.

Kaya was too streetwise when it came to stuff like that ever to trust what her eyes saw rather than what her brain said. Right now, her brain was telling her to get the lay of the land.

She duly made something and nothing noises about neighbours before falling silent.

'Talk to me,' Leo urged. 'You're tired and confused, but one thing you shouldn't be is afraid. Where have you been? Have you been away on holiday? Work? Visiting family—a boyfriend?'

They had begun to walk out into the hall and down the stairs, then back on themselves to the spacious, warm kitchen that faced extensive fields and land behind.

Kaya pushed open the kitchen door, switched on the light and looked around at a space that was no longer hers. She watched as he moved with confidence to one of the cupboards and reached for a couple of squat glasses to pour them both something amber-coloured and neat.

'I went to New Zealand to visit my mother,' Kaya said, backing away as he approached and sitting on one of the chairs at the kitchen table. Her voice was level and polite, her dark eyes watchful and guarded, noting everything about him—from the way he moved to the rich, golden colouring of his skin and the hard, cool contours of his extraordinarily handsome face. 'She moved there a few years ago when she remarried. I...needed to get away after Julie Anne's sudden death.'

'Julie Anne...' Leo murmured, shielding his dark gaze. 'And you returned to this house because...?'

'Because this is where I happen to have been living for the past three-and-a-half years.'

'Living here? You've been *living* here?'

'That's right.'

Leo hadn't seen *that* coming, but then again from a million miles away the situation had seemed pretty straightforward.

A letter had come from nowhere and it had blown a hole in his extremely controlled and highly regulated life. A buried past had resurfaced in the form of an inheritance from the woman who had dumped him into foster care at birth.

Leo had sat back and read the contents of that letter with bitterness, tempted to shred it and dispose of it in the bin. He had gazed around him, taken in the opulence of his New York penthouse apartment, one of several uber-luxurious apartments he owned in the various cities where his companies were based, and pondered the life he had conquered without the help of his flesh and blood, who had seen fit to get rid of him as a baby.

Memories he had locked away had resurfaced. He thought back to his young self, getting older in the nice enough foster home outside Brooklyn where he had been a number amongst other unwanted numbers. He'd thought back to the hopes and dreams of being rescued by his mum or dad gradually fading away, until steel had settled in his soul as he'd accepted the permanence of his surroundings.

He'd get out. He'd rule the world. He would become invulnerable.

And he had. He had worked longer, harder and with more determination than everyone else. He'd got into Harvard a year younger than everyone else and had breezed through a first in law, then moved on to get an MBA, and thereafter the world had been at his fingertips. He had joined a failing company with potential, bargained his way into being paid in shares and made a fortune when he had helped it go public.

He had been twenty-four.

He was thirty-one now and his fortune had multiplied so many times in the ensuing years that he was where he had always planned to be—on top of the world, occupying a place where he was untouchable.

Yet all of that success had faded in the face of that unexpected letter. His mother was dead and he was the beneficiary of everything she possessed, left to him by the woman who had given him up—some kind of token gesture to buy her way past the pearly gates. He had no time for that. It had been way too late for a guilty conscience.

'So you were saying…?' he drawled, shaking himself free from inconvenient trips down memory lane. 'You lived here with Julie Anne…'

'I did.'

Kaya heard the cold cynicism in his voice and stiffened, because whatever secrets her friend had concealed there could be no denying her warmth and generosity of spirit.

'How did that come about?'

Kaya shrugged. 'I returned from university, had nowhere to stay and couldn't afford the rent, at least not to start with. It's expensive here, with it being so close to Whistler.'

'And so this woman decided to step in and fill the gap, no questions asked?'

'I had known her since I was a kid so, yes, there were no questions asked. There were no strings attached to the offer. I wasn't made to rise at five and sweep floors until I collapsed.'

'Very generous of her.'

'She was a generous person,' Kaya said quietly. 'She was kind and sympathetic.'

Leo looked at her in silence for such a long time that she had to resist the temptation to squirm.

He was here to claim his inheritance but what was he going to do with it?

She was gripped by a sudden urgency to find out. Julie Anne had spent her life building up the halfway house, a place for women with nowhere left to turn. Was he here to demolish that legacy?

The lawyers had told her, briefly and as a courtesy, that he had been given up for adoption. That had been shocking in itself, but there would have been reasons behind that, even though Kaya had no idea what those reasons might be and had thought would never find out. Actions always spoke louder than words and

Julie Anne's actions had been those of someone with a big heart and a generous spirit.

But now she could feel the tide shifting, and anxiety clawed through her, because this guy was hard as nails. Exhaustion was beginning to catch up with her.

'You're asking a lot of questions,' she said coolly. It was hard to keep her eyes trained on him, because he made her feel uncomfortable, but she managed to maintain a level stare, not that he looked fazed by that.

'I have a right to. You asked me how I got into this house...'

'And now I know.'

Leo's eyebrows shot up and Kaya tilted her chin at a belligerent angle.

'You're the son, aren't you? You're the son who's come to get rid of all of this.'

CHAPTER TWO

KAYA SURFACED THE following morning, groggy and disoriented. For a few seconds, blinking in the darkness like an owl, she half-expected to glance to her left and see the landscape of pastoral Kiwi paradise through the bank of windows—rolling green fields undulating like gentle ocean waves, dotted with grazing sheep. Instead, what she saw was the steady fall of snow, fat, white flakes, and the dull, leaden skies of an unusually bleak Canadian winter.

And events of the night before came rushing back with the force of a freight train, barrelling into her at full pelt. The not-so-prodigal son had returned ahead of schedule, a hand grenade thrown through the window before she'd had time to batten down the hatches.

He'd been startled that she knew who he was and had wanted to pursue the conversation, but she had suddenly been overwhelmed. Overwhelmed by the shock of finding Julie Anne's son in the house. Overwhelmed by a future she hadn't got round to making provisions for suddenly slamming into her with the ferocity of a freight train. As much as anything else, overwhelmed by sheer exhaustion, hours and hours without sleep and everything catching up with her in one fell swoop. She'd had to get away from his stifling presence and, in fairness, he hadn't tried to stop her.

'Morning's as good a time to pick up this conversation,' he had ground out, watching her with an expression she had found disturbing for lots of reasons, and on cue she had fled.

She sat up and closed her eyes for a moment. *What the heck was going to happen now?*

While she'd been busy sorting her crazy thoughts out on the other side of the world, trying to come to terms with Julie Anne's sudden death, the legacy of truths she had withheld and the secrets she had concealed, Kaya had spared little time for the practicalities of having to vacate a house.

The lawyers had told her that these things could take a very long time to conclude and somehow she had mentally translated that as 'no need to rush…no need to start looking for somewhere else to live immediately…'

She was someone who had spent a lifetime being sensible and now it felt as though she was being punished for this one time when her common sense had temporarily deserted her. Her mind had been in a different place when she'd escaped to New Zealand, and the consequences of taking her eye off the ball had come home to roost. Now she felt exposed and vulnerable, two things she absolutely hated feeling.

She got dressed at speed, flinging on some jeans, a tee-shirt, a thick jumper and some winter socks. It was after ten in the morning although, as she yanked back the curtains, she thought anyone would be forgiven for thinking that it was still early because the skies were thick and dark with driving snow, and the placid spread of open land, stretching out to the majestic backdrop of mountains, was barely visible through the rapidly falling sheet of white.

She walked into the kitchen in under half an hour to find Leo already there, and she screeched to a halt in the doorway and felt her pulse speed up.

She'd somehow conveniently blanked out the sheer physicality of the man but she couldn't blank it out now.

He turned to look at her and their eyes met and held, tangled in a tense stretching silence. In the cold, thin, unforgiving light pouring through the bay windows that gave onto the front lawns, he was as sinfully beautiful as she now remembered. Long, lean, muscular, and in black jeans and black polo-neck, he looked every inch… *Every inch what?*

Every inch some kind of tycoon. Was that what he was—a tycoon? Or had he already started spending his unexpected inheritance?

'Slept well? Refreshed and ready to resume where we left off?'

Silence broken. Pulses racing all over the place, Kaya dragged her eyes away from the guy who had now unhurriedly turned to pour her a mug of coffee, making her feel like a stranger in her own home. Not that this was her home.

Kaya warily moved to one of the kitchen chairs. Out of the corner of her eye, she watched in thickening silence as he took his time with the coffee before bringing it to her and then sitting within touching distance. For a big man, he moved with an easy, stealthy grace that was compelling.

'Two sugars—plenty of milk. No idea how you take your coffee, but I feel it better to make it sweet just in case your blood sugar levels have dropped after last night.

'So, you knew who I was.'

'When did you get here?'

'Irrelevant. I'm thinking that your hysterical reaction to my presence in the bedroom was feigned, considering you were expecting me.'

'The lawyers contacted me. They said that Julie Anne had left everything to you.' Kaya lowered her eyes and felt the familiar clammy feel of bewilderment and betrayal at events she hadn't expected.

'Must have come as a body blow, considering you were living here with her.'

Kaya's mouth tightened and she flashed him an icy, hostile glare. 'I had no expectations.'

'Excellent news.'

'They told me that it would take a while for everything to get processed.'

'Why didn't you say anything? Why didn't you tell me that you knew who I was?'

'I wanted to wait and see what you had to say.'

For a couple of seconds, Leo was stuck for a response, because that would have been very much what he would have done if the boot had been on the other foot—waited and seen, and in the meantime have given nothing away.

He felt a tug of curiosity because a woman who gave nothing away was as rare as hen's teeth in his experience. Disconcerted, he frowned and then carried on, his voice as smooth as silk.

'To get back to what you just said...'

She wanted to wait to see what he had to say...

Leo sidelined his momentary lapse of self-control and focused. 'Under normal circumstances, I expect that would be the case. However...' He dealt her a slow, slashing smile that brought hectic colour to her cheeks. 'Money talks, and I have a lot of it. I wanted to get this situation wrapped up as soon as possible and they fast-tracked the procedure.'

'This situation...'

Leo shrugged. 'Came as much of a shock to me as it did to you. I never expected to be sitting here trying to sort out an inheritance that came from nowhere. You asked me when I got here? Less than two days ago so, as it turns out, it was just a matter of bad luck that you arrived shortly after I did, and even worse luck that we're snow bound. I'm sure you don't want to be here with me any more than I want to be here with you. Truth is, I could have got my people to deal with this but I felt it would probably be more suitable for me to handle it, given the circumstances.'

With every cold, passing word, Kaya could feel her tension building. The picture was slowly coming together in her head. The baby Julie Anne had given up for adoption had gone on to make a fortune and had returned as beneficiary of her estate, to dismantle it.

The prospect of that made her go cold.

Never mind *her*. What was going to happen

to the halfway house? The halfway house which had been a godsend to so many young, pregnant girls over the years and was part of the community. It had seen girls come, go and move on to bigger, brighter futures. It had sheltered them from storms that had blown away, given them a springboard to move on with their lives.

Kaya had done the books for the lodgings ever since she had graduated. She'd done voluntary work there since she'd been a teenager. Now this stranger was here, a dark intruder however entitled he was to Julie Anne's holdings, and what was he going to do with...with *everything*?

'I think I need something to eat.' She stood up but for the first time she hesitated, aware that this was no longer her house. He wasn't the stranger. *She* was.

'Feel free.'

He made an expansive gesture and then relaxed back to sip his coffee, watching her over the rim of the cup and sensing her uncertainty, although he had no intention of easing it. He wasn't here to make friends and influence people. He was here to get rid of whatever he'd inherited. He didn't expect to find answers to anything and he was mystified by the tug of curiosity that had brought him here in the first place.

'I haven't moved anything,' he drawled. 'The usual stuff is in the usual places.'

'Are you *enjoying* this?' Kaya moved to stand directly in front of him, hands on her hips, but almost immediately regretted it, because the sheer force of his presence and his ridiculous good looks made her feel unsteady.

'I'm here to do a job. Enjoyment doesn't enter into it.'

She had dressed in a hurry in some faded blue jeans, an equally faded jumper with no make-up, and her hair looked as though she had hurriedly run her fingers through it.

And yet her beauty transcended the lack of effort to promote it.

This was a sight to which Leo was unaccustomed. Cut to the chase: maybe he was enjoying a *tiny* part of it. The part of a red-blooded man appreciating the sight of a beautiful woman.

Not that he hadn't had his fair share of beautiful women. He had. Sexy women who aimed to please and were excellent when it came to stroking his ego. In a high-octane life, who didn't enjoy the calming influence of a soothing, agreeable woman?

This particular woman was scowling. He wondered if she was ever soothing and agreeable but then concluded that she probably was, just not with him. And who in his right mind could blame her?

He watched as she stalked off to the cupboard and fridge, but there was a self-conscious hesitancy as she fetched out whatever she wanted and, as much as that wasn't his concern, he actually felt a twinge of sympathy for the woman because this was not what she had expected.

'I could do something for you,' Kaya said grudgingly and Leo's eyebrows shot up.

'You make the offer sound so tempting.'

'I'm here, and I don't suppose it's any extra effort. It's just bread and jam.'

'Thank you but I'll make do with the coffee. I'm a guy who doesn't need breakfast on a daily basis.'

Kaya shrugged. She wasn't looking at him but his image was lodged in her head, and she was conscious of his eyes on her as she did some toast for herself, using the butter and jam he had bought and resenting him for crashing into her space without giving her the time or opportunity to take evasive action.

When she sat down, she made sure to position herself squarely in the chair furthest from him.

'What do you intend to do with the house and the land and…everything else?'

'"Highest bidder" are the two words that come to mind.'

'Why?' Kaya bit down on a piece of toast and resisted the temptation to launch into an argument with him because, if she faced it, she was in a weak position. How could she angle the conversation in a direction that might persuade him to think otherwise?

'Why would I hang on to all of this?' Leo stretched out his long legs and settled further into the chair to look at her over the rim of his cup as she sipped her coffee.

'You don't need the money,' she returned bluntly.

'Where are you going with this?'

'You said that you've got enough money of your own so why does it matter whether you sell this or not?'

'Are you suggesting that I hand the lot over to you?' Leo burst out laughing. 'Don't get me wrong, I understand that you're taken aback by my premature arrival on the scene, but I've never believed in Father Christmas and I definitely won't be auditioning for the role now. I have no use for any of the stuff my erstwhile birth mother decided to leave me for reasons I can't begin to fathom, but I won't be handing it over to you as a gesture of good will.'

'You're really not a very nice person, are you?' Kaya said through gritted teeth and, when he met her impotent fury with a grin, she had to clench her fists to stop herself from flinging her plate at his handsome head. 'I'm not interested in trying to persuade you to give me this house!'

'Good. Then we're on the same page.'

'There's more to Julie Anne's inheritance than bricks and mortar.' She pushed the plate away. The toast tasted like cardboard and there was a tight knot in her stomach because the guy sitting opposite her was as implacable as granite. Yet more than anything she wanted him to at least try and see her point of view.

Leo stilled.

Did he want to talk about the woman who had given birth to him and then promptly seen fit to dump him in foster care? No.

'Why did you bother to come here?'

'Come again?' His voice, though silky smooth, was laced with warning. Leo was a guy who had always been very clear when it came to boundaries. They were not meant to be stepped over—not by anyone. He was outraged at the open defiance in her dark eyes as she stared at him, her head tilted to one side, not backing down and certainly not intimidated.

'You're not interested in any of this, so why are you here? You said you could have sorted it out long-distance, so why didn't you? I mean, you made the effort to trek all the way here from your billionaire pad, or wherever, so the least you could is…is…'

The ground in front of her shimmered. She knew from the hard, cold expression on his face that she was entering no-go territory, and yet how would she be able to express her point of view if she backed away? If she took Julie Anne out of the equation, then this legacy went beyond her—it was bigger than her and bigger than both of them, and she was determined to let him know that—however it was clear that he just wasn't interested.

She would never forgive herself if the halfway house was dismantled, sold to the highest bidder and to heck with all the young girls who depended on it—the girls who had come and gone and who would come and go in the future.

'You're treading on thin ice here,' Leo said with menacing softness.

In response, Kaya stuck her chin out with more defiance, although she felt a whoosh inside her, a tingle of excitement as she met the cool challenge in his eyes.

This guy was like no one she had ever met in her life before but, then again, how many men had she met before? When it came to the opposite sex, she employed a strict 'hands off' policy because it was important for her to get to know a guy before she even thought about committing to anything like a relationship with him.

She'd learnt from experience, from watching the heart-breaking fallout of her mother's attempts to find love, that throwing oneself into relationships without the benefit of due diligence beforehand never worked.

Unfortunately, it was uneasy to acknowledge that the result of all that caution over the years had resulted in no relationship to speak of. No one had ever quite managed to get through Kaya's checklist.

She wasn't being fussy, she always told herself, she was simply *being careful*. But having had no men left gaping holes in her experience and right now, confronted with this guy, she was at a loss as to how to manoeuvre.

He was a powerful, mesmerising force of nature for which she felt lamentably ill-prepared. There was knowing experience in his dark eyes that made her horribly self-conscious and the way he smiled, the brooding intensity of his gaze, brought her out in goose bumps.

And worst of all was the simmering excitement that accompanied those goose bumps, a titillating sensation of stepping a little too close to an open flame that might be beautiful but was also lethally dangerous.

'Why?' She couldn't meet his stare full-on

and she briefly lowered her eyes and licked her lips. She breathed in deeply and looked at him once again but her heart was thumping like a sledgehammer inside her. 'I just want to find out why you bothered to come if you're so uninterested in finding out a bit more about your mother's legacy.'

'I don't believe I'm hearing this!' Leo said with outraged incredulity. 'Are you actually questioning my motives? What business is it of yours, exactly, what I intend to do about my so-called mother's legacy?'

'Because it matters.'

Leo vaulted upright. He was hanging onto his control with difficulty. His normal cool, calm composure had deserted him; but were her questions really so astonishing given the fact that, yes, he had made the choice to come here personally when there had been no real need? He was rich and he didn't need to accumulate any property from anyone to add to his portfolio so, that being the case, why bother with the formalities?

He knew that he hadn't lost his composure because she'd asked one or two reasonable questions. He'd lost his composure because she'd ignored his *Do Not Trespass* sign. The truth was that he had his rules and they were intractable. He had worked hard to be in control of his des-

tiny and there was a core of ruthless steel inside him that had propelled him over obstacles
and barriers that would have brought most other
men to their knees.

In return, he had come to accept a level of
untouchability that was never questioned, and
the mere fact that it was being questioned now
left him speechless.

Why did Julie Anne's legacy matter? What
difference would it make to this life? Would it
answer any questions, send his thoughts about
his past in another direction? No.

'She had plans for this house.'

'What are you talking about?'

If it had been seven in the evening, he would
have helped himself to something stiff and po-
tent but, as alcohol wasn't on the cards, he instead made himself another cup of coffee, black
and strong.

When he eventually looked at Kaya, when
their eyes met, he knew that his expression was
as unrevealing as it always was and that his
thoughts were hidden from view.

'You know about the halfway house…?'

'It's included in the paperwork. But forget
about that. You need to give this one up.'

'I can't.'

'What do you mean you *can't*?'

'Julie Anne…'

'Just for the record, dumped me in a foster home so I'm just going to put it out there that that's not exactly the behaviour of someone deserving of admiration. So why are you fighting her corner now?'

'Because I knew her.'

Leo was silenced by those four words. This was a woman who had known his mother, the very mother who had wanted nothing to do with him. A tangle of emotion surged through him and he scowled.

'Really…? You sure about that…?'

Kaya flushed but stood her ground. 'She… kept things from me, yes. Things from all of us, from everyone who knew her.'

'Everyone who thought they knew her,' Leo clarified politely.

'But that doesn't mean that the person we knew wasn't kind and generous and incredibly *good*. Because she was.'

'That's touchingly loyal, but where are you going with it?'

'If you've read through the stuff they sent you, then you'll have read something about the place she set up a long time ago. The halfway house.'

'I got rudimentary information,' Leo said on a sigh. 'I didn't get a book with chapters and paragraphs.'

'Well,' Kaya said stoutly, 'If you'll let me explain—'

'Right now, I don't think I can stand another round of chit chat about a woman I didn't know from Adam.'

He stood up and moved to the window to look outside at sky that remained ominously dark as it continued to shed its burden of thick, white snow across an alien landscape.

It snowed in Manhattan—the winters could be as brutal as this—but there was an essential difference. In Manhattan, the streets and roads were cleared because people had to get to work. The glass towers remained open for business. Broadband continued to do its thing so communications weren't brought to a crashing stop because of the weather. And from his penthouse apartment, with its far-reaching three-hundred-and-sixty-degree views, he could survey the city he felt he owned with a drink in his hand, knowing that the weather would seldom prove too much of an inconvenience.

He spun round to look at her.

'The Internet's down.'

'Is it?' Kaya frowned and was momentarily disconcerted by the abrupt change of topic, but then why should she be surprised if he didn't want to dwell on anything she had to say? 'I don't suppose it's that surprising. Look at what's happening outside.'

'Some snow,' Leo remarked wryly. 'It's hardly Armageddon. It snows in New York as well, believe it or not, and yet against all odds the Internet keeps working.'

'The Internet will be up and running in the town,' Kaya told him. 'Out here, it tends to be a little more erratic when the weather's like this.'

Leo looked at her and for the first time wondered what the hell a young woman like the one glaring at him, a young and incredibly striking young woman, was doing here holed up in a house she didn't own. Weren't bright lights beckoning? Was there a boyfriend on the scene? Some significant other tying her to a place anyone might have thought she would have left a long time ago? Especially considering her mother had upped sticks and moved halfway across the world.

She was asking him about New York, as though curiosity had staged a battle against hostile silence and lost, and for the first time he felt a flare of amusement.

It was satisfying to know that he wasn't the only one who was curious. Where he lived was no big secret. She could look him up on the Internet and find out pretty fast that he was rich beyond words and lived in the centre of Manhattan in an apartment in the most prestigious post code. It was no big deal to tell her about his place as he compared it to the house in which he now found himself.

'I enjoy city life,' he murmured. 'I like looking out my floor-to-ceiling windows and observing what's going on down below—the hustle and the bustle, a living, breathing city alive with possibilities. I don't find it claustrophobic. Now this?' He nodded to his surroundings without taking his eyes off her face. '*This* I find claustrophobic, which leads me to wonder how it is that you don't as well.'

How had he done that? Kaya wondered. How had he managed to reveal nothing about himself, really, while steering the conversation neatly in her direction, asking a question that was flagrantly nosy under the pretext of expressing the sort of anodyne interest *she* had expressed?

How had he made her suddenly think about her life and the paths she had chosen to take? Had she planned to stay put after her mother had disappeared to New Zealand? Or had she simply followed the path of least resistance, liking the peace of being grounded after a lifetime being the grown-up and practically taking care of her mother, who had treated her more as a pal than a daughter?

She had settled into a routine, especially after she had moved in with Julie Anne. She had relished normality and perhaps even found a place in life where, for once, she had someone she looked on as a mother figure, for Julie Anne had been far more of a mother to her than her own had ever been.

It had been easy to drift along without having to make any monumental decisions. And when it came to men...

Had it been easier from that point of view as well? Had it been easier just to stick with what she knew—guys she had more or less grown up with? A crowd she was comfortable in? Had it been easier just to delay the whole business of dealing with her singledom? No one had come along who fitted the bill and that had been fine.

Leo's blunt question dredged all this up and she wished she hadn't opened the door to his curiosity.

As if to remind her of their confinement, she saw the snow through the window and shivered.

How long were they going to be cooped up here? Surely they couldn't tiptoe around one another indefinitely? She would have to use their enforced captivity to at least try and get him to see another point of view, to have some insight into the inheritance he had unexpectedly come into, but how?

Kaya shivered. When she looked at him, she could feel hot colour creeping into her cheeks, depriving her of her ability to talk, sucking the oxygen from the air and leaving her hot and bothered.

The last thing she wanted was to get into some kind of confession mode with this guy, yet there was a dangerous charisma about him that she found difficult to deal with.

'I mean,' he drawled lazily, 'Maybe there's someone else here pinning you down?'

'What are you talking about?' Kaya blinked and surfaced from her meandering, uncomfortable thoughts.

'Well...' he spread his hands wide '...your mother's left for the opposite side of the world, so I guess you would have been free to get out of here and explore what else was on offer. Unless, of course, there's a boyfriend somewhere in the background keeping you tied to the kitchen sink, so to speak? Why else would you bury yourself out here, in the middle of nowhere with only an old woman for company?'

Kaya gasped because she found every single word he had just said offensive but, when she opened her mouth to tell him exactly what she thought of his commentary on her life, he burst out laughing.

'My apologies,' he said, although he was still

grinning, 'I'm not that much of a dinosaur to think that the role of any woman is tied to a kitchen sink…but my curiosity was genuine. What has kept you here?'

And just like that Kaya realised that he was the first person ever to have posed that question. Not even her mother had asked her and neither had Julie Anne nor any of her friends. None had ever wondered out loud how it was that she had decided to stay put when she had all the qualifications to forge a different, more adventurous life for herself somewhere else.

'You okay?'

'Of course. Why shouldn't I be?' She shot him a stiff, remote smile but her heart was pounding and there was something a lot like self-pity welling up inside her. And, alongside that self-pity, sheer frustration that a simple question from a guy she didn't even like had managed to raise questions she didn't particularly want to answer, had thrown her into a stupid tailspin.

She gathered herself.

'I like open spaces,' she said, thankful that her voice sounded normal. At any rate, that wasn't a lie, although it did jostle uncomfortably close to truths she didn't care to confront. 'I grew up in Alaska until I was six before moving here. I would go mad if I had to live somewhere like New York.'

'You lived in Alaska? So—'

'So there's Internet in the town,' Kaya cut in before he could embark on another line of questioning. She stood up and moved towards the old-fashioned sink and then stood there, facing him, her hand firmly placed on the counter behind her. 'It must be inconvenient for you, being here and cut off from your work. If we clear the snow, you should be able to make it into town. Once you get to the main road, it'll be a lot more passable.'

And in the meantime, she thought, she wasn't going to let him get under her skin. *In the meantime*, she was going to engineer the conversation in the direction *she* wanted. She didn't have time on her side when it came to ramming her point of view down his throat, and she had no intention of wasting it by breaking out in a hot sweat every time he looked at her.

She was pleased to be back in command of herself. 'If we get a head start, then it can be all systems go when this snow decides to ease off.'

CHAPTER THREE

THE LEADEN GREY skies of the day before were now a washed out, denim blue and the snow had collected everywhere and on everything even though it seemed to be giving up the fight, diminishing to whipping flurries.

There were no houses around, nothing to interrupt an unbroken vista of white. Leo looked at the woman who had started attacking the build-up of snow with even, rhythmic movements—spade in, flick, spade out—at home clearing a path, accustomed to doing this year in and year out.

No boyfriend… No family, he assumed… No ties except those bred through familiarity, old friends and maybe from her school days. A comfortable, unchallenging life, which sounded pretty good if you happened to be retired.

Frankly, he didn't get it.

Her back story didn't matter, and it certainly didn't make a scrap of difference when it came to doing what he had come to do, but it was certainly adding a little vim and vigour to the situation, stuck out here.

'You were telling me about Alaska.'

'Are you going to help shovel snow or are you going to stand there, leaning on the spade and doing nothing?'

Leo grinned. He didn't know many women who would be out in these conditions clearing snow and he didn't think it was a crime to appreciate the sight of one now.

She had changed into her thickest winter gear—jumpers, waterproof jacket and waterproof trousers tucked into serviceable knee-high wellies. Her woolly hat was pulled low over her ears and her gloves were thick enough to withstand snow storms with no threat of frostbitten fingers.

'I'm appreciating the scenery.'

About to plunge her shovel into the snow, Kaya paused to look at him and her heart skipped a beat. He was staring straight at her and she felt heat begin to spread through her, a lick of fire racing through her veins and turning on a switch she'd never known existed.

He had come prepared for the cold. He wore thick, dark layers, serviceable waterproof, fur-lined boots, a black waterproof oilskin coat and a black woolly hat. He looked sexy and dangerous and the way he was looking at her made her wonder whether there had been something flirtatious behind that innocent remark. No, surely not? Had there been? He didn't like her! She was taking up space in his house and she was an encumbrance to be rid of. So why would he flirt with her?

Panic flared, reminding her how innocent she was when it came to games like this. She just wasn't used to it, wasn't used to a man like the one staring at her, his dark eyes guarded and assessing.

She had never cut her teeth on all those youthful make-up and break-up teenage games her friends used to play. She had spent those years learning how pointless those games were, thanks to the example set by her mother. In many ways, she had felt smugly superior at the tears shed when boys had come and gone. She was saving herself for something serious and lasting, for the guy who wouldn't mess her around and break her heart. Except, she realised now, those gaps in her knowledge had made her vulnerable.

She stared at him, frozen and tongue-tied, then belatedly decided to take what he had said at face value and launched into a monologue about the countryside, the tourists that flocked to their pretty little town, an overspill from Whistler, and its skiing industry.

She knew that she was babbling and she could feel herself getting hotter and hotter under the collar. She could barely have a conversation with the man without breaking out in a sweat and she was infuriated with herself for her weakness. She'd always considered herself pretty strong, able to withstand anything and anyone, toughened by a background that had foisted responsibilities onto her shoulders at a young age. Yet right at this moment...

She needed to get a grip. She needed to be that cool, controlled person who could make a case for him not to throw Julie Anne's life work down the tubes because he had an axe to grind with the woman who had given him up for adoption.

Because that was what it came to, wasn't it? He was bitter and she couldn't blame him.

There was also a part of her that could be bitter, that could look back at her dear friend and harbour a grudge against her for keeping this huge secret to herself. But she didn't because she had the benefit of having known her for who she was, whatever secrets she had kept to herself.

He hadn't.

Calmed by that, Kaya resumed shovelling,

and out of the corner of her eye saw that he was working at it as well, except in his case he was getting an awful lot more done with a lot less effort.

Her eyes drifted to the flex of muscle just about discernible under the layers and she was riveted when he shrugged off the waterproof jacket and shoved up the sleeves of his dark jumper.

'Hot work,' he said without looking at her. 'Or maybe I'm just not used to a bit of honest manual labour.'

He glanced at her with amusement.

She was flushed, her cheeks pink, her mouth half-parted, as though he'd caught her on the verge of saying something.

'How long did you think you'd have here before I came on the scene?' he asked. Her eyes flew to his and widened.

'A couple of months,' Kaya admitted, looking away. 'If I thought you'd show up as soon as you did, I wouldn't have taken all that time out in New Zealand. I would have returned earlier so that I could sort myself out.'

'I don't plan on hanging on to any of this,' Leo said shortly. 'But I won't chuck you out without at least some notice.'

Kaya thought of the halfway house and the vulnerable girls who walked through those doors with nothing much aside from some hope for temporary respite. For many, it was a last resort. She was honour-bound to protect those girls. She had formed links with many of them over the years, just as Julie Anne had.

There was no place for emotions when it came to trying to save the place. She needed to get him on side. They needed to call a truce and, in fairness, she was the one who couldn't relax.

She hadn't noticed a car when she had arrived the evening before but, as they made inroads into the snow, she saw that he had indeed driven. There was a shiny, black, solid four-wheel drive parked at the side of the house alongside her old, reliable car which had survived many a heavy-duty winter.

'What do you do?' she asked.

'What do I do about what?'

'In life. I mean, what's your job?'

Leo followed her eyes, saw her clock his car and wondered whether he'd been mistaken when he'd spotted a look of something on her face, something fleeting that told him that the spectacle of something so obviously expensive didn't impress her. She was contemptuous of it.

'I own things.'

'What does that mean?'

'It means I built a life for myself without help from anyone.' He stuck the shovel into the snow and rubbed his gloved hands together. 'It means I pulled myself up by my boot straps and sorted my life out without the guiding hand of the friend you're so intent on defending. I buried my head in books, studied until I knew more than anyone else and battled against prejudice to make it to the top.

'I took risks without the benefit of any cushions lying around to break a fall. I gambled for high stakes and, every time I threw the dice, I knew that life could go one way or the other. All I had was faith in my own intelligence, instinct and knowledge of every market I decided to play. Now, I own the world. I have the freedom to do whatever I want and all of that was acquired without help.'

'I can't blame you for being bitter.'

'That's very generous of you.'

He shook his head and half-laughed at himself, because he wasn't given to self-pitying diatribes, but at least it should sound an alarm bell against any more forays into sermons about Julie Anne and the properties he really couldn't care less about.

'I think we've done enough to warrant a cup of coffee,' he said, moving to get his jacket but not bothering to put it on. 'Snow's stopped, at any rate. Augurs well for life returning to normal.'

'You're not the only one who's had it hard,'

Kaya said, keeping up with him but only just as they headed to the front door. She could feel her good intentions slipping through her fingers. How did she get through to someone who was so intransigent?

Watching him as he strode into the house and slung his jacket over one of the coat hooks by the front door brought home to her his ownership of this and of everything else that came with it.

'Did I ever say that I was?'

He glanced over his shoulder but he was back in control, a small, amused smile curving his mouth and not a trace of bitterness in evidence. He held her gaze for a few seconds, head tilted thoughtfully to one side.

'What have you got against rich guys?'

This came from nowhere and Kaya's mouth fell open as she stared at him.

'What are you talking about?' She began stripping off, because it was baking in the house, heating full-blast. She yanked off the woolly hat and shook her hair free, not looking at him as her waterproof joined his on the coat hook by the door and her boots got dumped underneath.

'I saw the way you looked at my car, Kaya. Same way I've caught you looking at me. So what's the problem here—is it just me? Is it me because I'm rich? Or is it rich guys in general? Can't be that you have a thing against money because...' he looked around him as he began strolling towards the kitchen '...this place and everything else that came as part of the package deal all point to a woman who had more than enough to keep going.'

'I—I don't know what y-you're talking about,' Kaya spluttered in response and he laughed and turned away, moving towards the kettle, flicking it on then getting out coffee, mugs and milk.

He owned the space around him. She wondered whether that was just who he was: a guy in charge, the sort of person who would have been as at home here if he'd walked in from the cold to find shelter. A man who was so utterly self-confident that he could have been dumped on another planet and he'd have started working out how he could make it his.

'Sure you do. Milk? Sugar? You know exactly what I'm talking about.'

'You think you're so observant.'

'I don't think. I *know*. Trust me, when you grow up in a foster home you learn how to look after yourself. You learn how to have eyes at the back of your head and how to hear through walls, because nobody in charge is going to be there twenty-four-seven doing that job on your behalf. And you learn fast how to watch people and work out what makes them tick. So, what's it about rich guys you don't like?'

He dumped a mug of hot coffee in front of her and then sat on the very same chair he'd been sitting on before they'd gone outside to deal with the snow.

He had stripped off the black jumper and was down to a long-sleeved, close-fitting tee shirt, also black, that emphasised the muscular body she had surreptitiously stared at when he'd been shovelling the snow.

'You don't look like her,' she said impulsively and Leo frowned, disconcerted. 'Julie Anne—you don't look like her. She was very blonde, very attractive. Blue eyes.' Her words dropped into the silence between them, spreading ripples of restless discomfort through her. He didn't like what she was saying. He'd come here to sort things out but he was happy to leave without knowing anything about his mother, without making any effort to try and understand the good woman she had been, whatever she had done all those years ago when she had been very young.

'I have pictures, if you want to see—on my phone. She hated having her photo taken but I sometimes managed to capture her when she wasn't looking, or else just told her that she had no choice. But in the house…you'd be hard pressed to find any. She just wasn't interested in seeing herself in photo frames on shelves. That's what she used to say—made me smile.'

'I'll pass.'

'Aren't you curious at all?'

'Let's park this,' Leo ground out, eyes cool. 'If I was interested in seeing pictures of Julie Anne, I'm pretty sure I would have been able to get hold of some by now.'

'You were asking me about rich guys,' Kaya said, her eyes as cool as his. 'And you're right. I don't have any time for men with money because they're all…arrogant and full of themselves. They swan around thinking they can do whatever they like, and enjoy snapping their fingers and watching people jump to their command.' She allowed a significant pause and his eyebrows shot up, not in anger, but in amusement.

'I'm guessing that's a dig at me.' He grinned. 'Is that what you think I've been doing? Swanning around and snapping my fingers so that I can watch you jump to my command? If that was my ploy, then I've failed miserably, because so far I haven't seen you doing a lot of jumping at my command. Anyway, isn't that all a bit of a generalisation? Or is your attitude something to do with the tough upbringing you were going to tell me about?'

He remembered...remembered she'd vaguely mentioned that he wasn't the only one who'd had it hard. The conversation hadn't been continued but her throwaway remark had lodged in his head, waiting for the right moment to be pulled out and examined further.

Of course, this was how he had got where he'd got, she thought. He was smart and she could believe it when he'd said that he'd had to work hard and take risks. But there would have been more to it than that because lots of people worked hard and took risks. He would have had that added edge to him of being street wise. He would have been the guy who stored things in his head, who knew how to hold on to information until an opportunity came for him to take advantage of what he knew.

'You really want to know?' Kaya was willing to drop her guard for a bit, to let him see a side of her she didn't normally share with anyone, because to get him at least to listen to her she surely had to see her for more than just a nuisance who kept asking questions he didn't want to answer? He had to see her as a three-dimensional person with a story to tell, something to engage his interest and make him look beyond what was on the surface.

'Try me.'

'My mother,' she said bluntly. She thought of

her mother and was taken back through time to when she had become old enough to understand that their relationship was not at all like the relationship her other friends had with their mums.

'My mum,' she said softly. 'My dad died when I was very young. You know…they were crazy about one another. I can't remember much about him, because I was only six when he died, but I remember them laughing a lot. She was always the extrovert. He was very quiet, very serious. She once told me that he was a complete nerd until he met her, said that she made him light-hearted and he anchored her.'

'How did he die?'

'He fell through what should have been solid ice while he was trying to install a system for tracking hibernating sea life under the ice. He was a marine biologist, and he specialised in icy water, because he'd grown up surrounded by it in Alaska. My mother was devastated. He hadn't been good with money, hadn't taken out any kind of life insurance, and without any property or possessions to speak of she was left with very little and a young child to look after. We moved here because this was my mother's home before she left it to go to Alaska with my father. She still had connections here, although no family.'

'And your learning curve…' Leo said slowly. 'She had no money and she…what?'

Their eyes met and she shot him a wry smile. 'You can maybe guess.'

'How did you deal with that?'

'You mean the ever-changing revolving door of cute rich men my mother hoped would put a ring on her finger and money in her bank account? It's like she went off the rails when she lost the love of her life. Every time one relationship ended, she would start looking for his replacement, and it was always easy to find one because she was so beautiful. No...my mum never had a problem finding guys. It was the keeping them that eluded her. The guys who used her were always rich and good-looking.'

'And you're lumping me in the same category? A rich guy who uses women?'

Kaya didn't say anything. She was surprised at how much she had confided and astonished at how heartfelt her confession had been. Had she been deluded into thinking that he was some sort of kindred spirit? Or had she become so accustomed to never opening up that opening up now was like releasing a dam? Perhaps the fact that he was a stranger helped. He would be in her life for ten minutes and then he would be gone for ever, so what was the danger in handing him some confidences?

'I don't see a wedding ring on your finger any more than you see one on mine,' she pointed out, ignoring his look of utter incredulity at the sheer brazen cheek of her having told him what she thought. Indeed she was tempted to laugh out loud at his expression.

'Is there someone lurking in the background?' She pulled the tail of the tiger and felt a rush of forbidden excitement, a stirring in her blood that was heady. 'I'm only saying what you said to me. Is there a girlfriend waiting for you in Manhattan? Maybe not tied to the kitchen sink because, like you told me, you're no dinosaur...'

'No, as a matter of fact!'

Leo raked his fingers through his hair and sat back to stare at her with an expression of outrage underscored with grudging admiration.

'You're a rich guy who plays the field because he can.'

'I can't believe I'm hearing this!'

Kaya wanted to tell him that his very reaction was proof positive of everything she had just said. He was the rich guy who pulled strings and never thought that he had to answer to anyone.

'I'm honest with the women I choose to go out with.' Leo slanted her a darkly brooding look from under his lashes, and Kaya shivered in automatic response to a stretching tension that felt oddly sensual. She knew that this was her inexperience coming to the surface again, undermining her composure and throwing her off-balance. Her one serious relationship, which had fizzled out over a year ago into a something and nothing kind of friendship, had definitely not prepared her for this assault on her emotions. Thoughtful, sensitive and considerate, whilst lovely on paper, had ended up being frustrating in reality and certainly hadn't come close to what this stranger evoked in her, which felt wild and reckless.

'What does that mean?' Her voice was low and breathy.

'It means I don't play games with them—with anyone. I don't string them along, and I wouldn't dream of using any woman. I'm sorry your formative years were spent witnessing your mother's mistakes but, whoever those guys were, they were nothing like me. Believe it or not, I pride myself on being a man of honour!'

'But not a man who's willing to listen to what other people have to say!'

'Meaning?'

'You've written off Julie Anne. You don't even want to know what she looked like, never mind what she was all about. You probably wouldn't care to know that she hoped to turn part of this house into select accommodation for girls from the halfway house when there's overspill. There's acres of land attached to this house. She was going to invest in some horses, something that could provide therapeutic enjoyment for girls who might feel that life is hopeless as they come to terms with pregnancies they're not equipped to handle. Surely you can see that maybe, just maybe, your mother was trying to atone for what she did?'

'Not this again!' He vaulted upright and moved to stand directly in front of her before leaning down, hands splayed on the arms of the chair on which she sat, his expression angry and impatient as he stared at her. He was so close that she could see the flecks of gold in his dark eyes and could breathe in the scent of him, musky and masculine.

'I haven't come here to rescue anything or anyone,' he snarled through gritted teeth. 'I'm going to sell the lot and return to Manhattan where I live, and the sooner the better. So all those bleeding-heart stories about your saintly friend? The very same saintly friend who dumped me thirty-two years ago? Not going to work. Atonement doesn't make up for crimes committed! Atonement is just a pointless, self-serving afterthought!'

He straightened but there was a sudden urgent restlessness in him that made the atmosphere between them electric. Kaya couldn't peel her eyes away from him. She could *feel* his energy, feel his impatience and ferocious disapproval of the way she had pushed back against him, but she refused to be cowed.

She stubbornly met his angry dark eyes until he rasped, 'I have to get out of here.'

'And go where?'

'You said there's Internet in the town somewhere. I need to work.'

'Are you going to *drive* in?'

'I'll walk. I damn well need the exercise.'

He spun round on his heels and jerkily prowled to the window to look through at the fields at the back of the house.

Tension radiated from his body in waves. She'd made no headway at all. All that rage and anger at a past he couldn't change would always stand in the way of him seeing beyond it to the good his mother had done.

By harping on, she had probably done the opposite of what she had intended, and she could feel defeat settle on her shoulders. There didn't seem anything left to say, so she was silent when he eventually turned to look at her.

'I'll be back when I'm back,' he told curtly. 'We'll discuss formal arrangements then—set a date for when you think you'll be able to vacate the property. If needs be, I can instruct my people to assist in finding you somewhere to live.'

'I'll manage,' Kaya said tautly. 'I'll make sure to start packing my things while you're gone.'

Their eyes clashed and she was the first to look away.

She didn't move but she heard the sound of his footsteps in the hall and then the slam of the front door.

She would start clearing her stuff. The snow had stopped and the sooner she cleared off, the better.

It was a while before Kaya peeped over the parapet. Her head was raging with helpless, fist-clenching, teeth-grinding frustration as she attacked her bedroom, sorting things into piles and discovering that there was a hell of a lot more stored in nooks and crannies than she'd expected.

That damn man was impossible!

His bitterness was insurmountable. He might have made his fortune and found his freedom, he might have had everything he'd ever wanted within his grasp, but none of that, obviously, had given him peace of mind.

He still seethed, and he would seethe for ever, because he would never find the answers to the questions he had probably asked himself over the years.

Why?

Why had he been given up?

Sitting back on her haunches amidst the chaos

of clothes dragged from drawers and cupboards, Kaya lost herself in contemplation of what he must have spent his lifetime going through and what he would be going through now. For it would surely have been rammed in his face that, whatever thoughts he had nurtured about his mother, they had not revolved around her being a decent, middle class, well-off do-gooder. That wasn't the stereotype of any woman who handed her baby up for adoption.

But did he imagine that he was alone in his bewilderment and hurt? Didn't he realise that she, as well, had questions that would now never be answered? Couldn't he see that she had been winded and knocked for six when she'd been told of his existence?

She didn't notice the passing of time until she glanced at her mobile to realise that it had gone five-thirty and he had been out of the house for *hours*. On foot and in unfamiliar territory.

She uneasily debated what to do. She didn't have his mobile number. How was she to contact him? Should she have tried to dissuade him from his crazy decision to walk into town? It was doable, she thought, chewing her lip, but was it doable when he didn't have the foggiest idea where he was going?

The snow had completely stopped, which was a good thing, but there were still piles of it everywhere, great, white drifts pale against the darkness. Piles of treacherous snow lying in wait for an unwary stranger.

Had he even made it to the town in one piece or was he lying somewhere in a ditch, waiting for help to show up? It would be easy to get lost in a place like this, where the snowy fields in winter could become a bewildering maze, and the stretching white mountains a series of lethal ledges and drops.

The man might get under her skin until she wanted to scream but she would never forgive herself if he ended up injured, or worse, because she had driven him to the end of his tether, forcing him to escape on a dangerous walk in unknown terrain.

She flew downstairs, slung on all the warm layers she had earlier discarded and felt the sharp cold on her as she let herself out of the house and headed to her car.

She knew this drive to town and could have done it blindfolded, but she was still forced to creep along at a snail's pace, because of the snow and because she was peering into the pools of darkness for an inert Leo at the side of the road.

The only up side to the tortuous trip was that there was no traffic at all. Only a lunatic would have been out in this part of the country on a night like this. As she edged towards the town, things picked up. Most of the shops were open. Lights glittered and there were people around, picking up groceries, stocking up on water just in case.

The town was a meandering network of charming streets that encircled a little park, now white and empty, and a church that was used throughout the year for all sorts of things. Retail parks and mega-stores still had to make it there and the atmosphere was of a place waiting for modern life to happen. But scratch the surface and, yes, there were Icafés with Wi-Fi, a gleaming shop that sold the most up-to-the minute ski equipment and boutiques where the rich and famous would not have felt uncomfortable.

And on the outskirts of the town, but within walking distance, were all sorts of houses, large and small, bordered with sloping front lawns that lazed under huge, sprawling trees. Settling snow would not have affected anyone living here.

Kaya found parking easily.

She hadn't been here since she'd left to see her mother two months ago and now she looked and appreciated what she'd left behind—the laid-back bustle, the spectacle of the snow on the roofs of the shops which turned the picturesque town into a postcard. The old-fashioned street lights that hadn't been changed in decades cast shadows across the pavements as groups walked by, soaking up the atmosphere and the beauty of thick snow.

She hit the first café at speed. She had no idea what she would do if she couldn't find Leo. Her thoughts were tangled and panicked, and underscored with guilt when she spotted him through the broad planes of glass that opened to a brightly lit space inside.

The first place! Whilst she had been wracked with fears of him wandering in a lost daze in a confusing white landscape, he had gaily made his way to the first café he had come across and set up camp!

There he sat, larger than life and cool as a cucumber! He was sprawled back on one of the low sofas, surrounded by a bevy of men and women, all young and all beautiful and, in the case of the women—five of them, to be precise—all agog with open admiration at whatever he was saying.

Panic turned to rage with supersonic speed. She forced herself to breathe slowly and evenly. She neared the window and peered inside. Should she just do an about turn and walk away, leaving him to make his own merry way back to the house? After all, hadn't he told her that he would be back when he was back? He hadn't asked her to start her own one-woman search party for him! And, besides, in record time he had found himself a fan club. One of them would no doubt snap up the opportunity to deliver him back to the house in one piece. They all looked as though they wanted to gobble him up!

She was swinging away when their eyes met.

His dark eyes pinned her to the spot through the laughing group and Kaya froze. She watched, resigned, as he slowly stood up, while his circle of groupies leapt to its feet in an apparent attempt to detain him. She decided that it was a very unedifying sight.

His eyes never left her face, even when he was making a song and dance of ruefully taking his departure.

She should never have let guilt get the better of common sense. She should have remembered the way he had stormed out, immune to listening to anything she had had to say. Did he have any scruples when it came to saying exactly what he thought? No. He did as he pleased, and behaved exactly how he wanted to behave without the slightest need to obey common rules of courtesy and listen to her.

He wasn't interested in the case she was making for the sake of the retreat Julie Anne had set up, and he didn't see any reason why he had to pretend to show interest. He was the very epitome of the guy he claimed not to be—so rich that he could do as he pleased and then make pointless excuses for his bad behaviour.

The closer he got, the angrier she became and, by the time the glass door to the café swung open and he sauntered towards her, she was ready to combust.

CHAPTER FOUR

HE HADN'T EXPECTED to see her. He'd left the house more wired than he'd ever been in his life.

She'd wanted to open up his eyes to an up-lifting vision of all the good work Julie Anne had spent her life doing. She'd wanted him to get past the annoying technicality of his abandonment and look beyond it, to the woman who had decided to seek atonement doing whatever it was she'd done, paving the way for young girls who needed shelter.

She'd wanted him to forgive and forget.

Never had he felt such a surge of bitterness as the old feelings he'd thought he'd laid to rest had returned with devastating force.

He'd had to leave.

Unaccustomed to any loss of control, the rush of emotions overwhelming him, threatening to take him back to a dark place he'd left behind, had been too much. But, even as he'd fought against the snow to make his way into town, with the silence of the night a calming companion, he'd recognised that the woman hadn't said any of the things to rile him.

More than that, he'd been forced to concede that he wasn't the only one with unresolved issues on the subject of his mother.

Yes, he'd had years living with what she'd done, but she'd also seemed to have done a number on Kaya, a person who had loved and trusted her. She'd kept him a secret—surely that would eat away at the memories she had of her friend? Yet, somehow, she had transcended any disappointment or disillusionment and had been determined to give Julie Anne the benefit of the doubt.

He, on the other hand, could not be quite so forgiving.

He'd been glad of the arduous, freezing walk, which had calmed him, and he'd found the café without any trouble. By the time he'd reached civilisation, he'd been more than happy to ditch the work he had resolved to do and immerse himself in the sort of superficial laughter and bonhomie that came as second nature to him.

That he could handle. It was easy to weave that magnetic spell over people, easy to join in, seemingly charming and mesmerising while deep inside he held himself back, always watching from the outside, participating but only so much and no more.

With Kaya and her questions and searching dark eyes…? Well, it seemed ridiculously difficult and he wondered whether it was because of a connection throbbing between them, one he hadn't instigated but one that was there nevertheless.

The connection of his mother.

Kaya made a mockery of his self-control and that, as much as anything else, he had wanted to escape.

But he hadn't expected to look through those panes of glass out into a lamp-lit street to see her standing there looking, it had to be said, livid.

The sharp satisfaction he had felt the minute he had spotted her defied common sense. Just like that, earlier frustrations vanished and his equanimity returned, stabilising him and bringing a small smile to his lips as he joined her outside in the freezing cold.

'This is unexpected,' he drawled. 'To what do I owe the pleasure?' Next to Kaya, scowling and glaring, all those attractive young women he had just been chatting with faded into oblivion.

Under the street lamps, her exotic beauty was thrown into sharp relief. He felt a kick of sexual awareness and drew in a sharp breath.

'You were gone for hours,' Kaya said through gritted teeth, stalking towards her car, not sparing him a glance and absolutely regretting every guilt-ridden twinge that had propelled her into getting behind the wheel to seek him out.

When she thought of the way she had anxiously peered left and right, scouring the verges *just in case*, only to spot him flirting away with a bunch of women in the café, she wanted to grind her teeth in frustration.

'My apologies if you were worried.'

'Who said anything about being worried?'

As she yanked open the car door, he could see the tinge of colour in her cheeks. She tugged her hair and he noted the slight trembling of her fingers. And she was *still* studiously avoiding his eyes.

Because…what?

Because she was *aware* of him? Because underneath her annoyance she was as aware of him on a basic, primal level as he was of her?

Leo didn't get it. This wave of incomprehensible attraction he felt when he was near her was so unusual for him.

Was it down to the extraordinary nature of their meeting? Or was it because she was just so different from the sort of women he went out with, dated and slept with? She demanded, she ignored his barriers, she challenged him and then stuck to her guns even when he signalled to her to back off. He shouldn't have found any of that alluring but, against all odds, he did.

Was it the pull of novelty? The truth was that he had never sought out a woman like Kaya. He wasn't and never had been interested in cultivating long-term relationships with anyone. He didn't do love because he didn't believe in it. What examples had he ever had of a loving relationship? His own flesh and blood had not been able to love him and surely that should be love in its purest form? Surely that should be love that lacked self-concern, the most selfless love of all? And if he had never experienced that, if that had been too tough for a couple of feckless parents to master, then what hope for the complicated, gruelling business of love that was based on attraction, hope and belief in fairy-tale nonsense about happy-ever-afters?

No; in his head, love was pain and loss and in ways that he couldn't put his finger on. He had come to accept that it was an emotion he would never allow himself to feel.

So, if he went for relationships that were transitory and superficial, then that was just fine with him because he wasn't interested in anything beyond that.

Part of him acknowledged that in going for a certain type of woman, for laying down boundaries that he insisted be adhered to, he was taking the route he knew to be safe, the route that would protect his heart.

He had never envisaged feeling any sort of sexual pull to a woman who demanded more from him than what was straightforward.

So Kaya? It was baffling.

But right now, as that telling colour remained staining her cheeks, there was certainly something about this inexplicable tug, something that made his blood hot and suffused him with a sort of keen, restless craving that was utterly novel and disturbing.

But also quite exciting.

'If you weren't worried, you wouldn't have bothered,' Leo pointed out reasonably. 'If I recall, you weren't exactly the height of warm and friendly when I decided to head to town.'

'Can you blame me?'

'Really want to go down this road again? Because I don't.'

Kaya slanted a glance at him and bristled. The man could not have got on her nerves more and yet she was still so aware of him next to her as they bounced along back to the house, driving back to it slightly faster than she had come from it.

He'd left the house with an angry slam of the front door but he couldn't be in a more chipper mood now. That was what a fan club of pretty young things could do for a guy, she thought sourly, and then was immediately impatient with herself for the thought.

Fact was, she was the only one fuming here. He was cool, calm and collected. He'd made up his mind and he wasn't going to start having second thoughts. If she ventured into that slice of forbidden territory again, then there was no telling how hard he would slam the door in her face.

And the truth was that she still had a load of clearing out to do, including Julie Anne's quarters, which she had left as was when she'd disappeared off to New Zealand. At the time, she'd been far too shaken to undertake that heart-wrenching task.

They were going to be sharing space for at least another twenty-four hours and low-level sniping was going to be exhausting.

Thinking rationally was one thing, though. Putting it into practice was quite another when the guy sitting next to her was making her feel as though she were on the verge of going up in flames.

'I had no idea whether you'd become disoriented out there,' she said in a driven undertone. 'You don't know this part of the world and I wanted to make sure you hadn't fallen in a ditch.'

'I've always been very good at navigating my way in places I don't know.'

'So I've seen,' Kaya muttered. 'You certainly managed to navigate your way to a jolly crowd of friends in no time at all.'

'What can I say? People like me.' He paused. 'With one or two exceptions.'

'Do you think this is funny?'

'What?'

Kaya's head was bursting. Everything was rushing at her all at once. Seeing him there in that café, laughing and joking... Somehow it had brought home to her the life she led—a careful, responsible life; the life of someone who didn't hang out in cafés laughing and giggling with the cute new guy in town.

He had swept in on a blizzard of snow and everything was upside down now. She had been forced to face limitations within herself that she hadn't faced before. How entrenched had she become in a life that held few surprises and stretched ahead of her without the excitement of anything unknown?

If her mother had been the 'naughty one', then how easy had it been for her to over-compensate by being the good girl?

And did *good girls* have fun?

Somewhere along the line, had she ended up equating fun with being like her mother—irresponsible, throwing herself into untenable relationships…getting hurt over and over again?

She resented the fact that Leo had opened her eyes to all this murky stuff. But more than that she resented the fact that, despite it all, she still couldn't stop her body from responding to him. She still couldn't sit next to him in a banged-up old four-by-four without this electric thread of sexual awareness running through her veins.

Because that was what this was. It wasn't just an objective appreciation of a guy who was sinfully good-looking. This was the sort of attraction that she had never before felt in her safe, guarded, carefully thought-out life.

And there he sat, refreshed after socialising at the café, not a care in the world.

She pulled into the still snowy drive that wound its way up to the house with reckless abandon, barely aware of the slide of the four-wheel drive as it shuddered to an uneven stop.

'Everything!' she said. 'None of this is funny.' She stared at him and there was a stretching silence. It went on and on and on. She could feel her temples begin to throb.

'No. None of it is.'

Kaya stared at him. It was dark out here and she could feel the cold collecting around them, trying to find a way past her layers. His eyes were dark and glittering and he was looking at her with deadly seriousness. Suddenly the confines of the car felt very, very oppressive and the atmosphere had become electric.

Her eyes widened. When she drew in a sharp breath, she almost couldn't release it, and when she did it was on a wrenched shudder.

'You don't understand,' she whispered. 'I don't know what to do. This is all I've ever known. Okay, I knew I'd have to leave the house—I accepted that. But I just thought I'd have time to come to deal with it.'

'I told you, I'm not going to force you to pack your bags and leave first thing.'

'I still have so much clearing left to do. I never realised how much could accumulate in the space of a handful of years, and I haven't even begun to go through Julie Anne's rooms yet.'

'That's the locked room?'

'She has a suite. She liked pottering there—watching telly and doing admin. It's cluttered. I still have to go through her things, and it's going to be awful.'

She broke eye contact but her heart thudded painfully inside her and she gripped the steering wheel for dear life.

For the first time since he'd appeared in her

life, changing *everything*, Kaya felt the prick of tears behind her eyes. All the arguments, all the determination to try and get him to appreciate the legacy he had inherited, had leeched out of her and she was left feeling hollow inside.

She felt his hand cover hers and heat washed over her. She looked down at his hand and then at him. She didn't want to move because she didn't want him to take his hand away. She liked the heat of it burning through her jacket, jumper and the million and one layers underneath.

It was a shameful acknowledgement and it left her feeling weak. It left her feeling…as if she wanted more. More than just his consoling hand on hers, more than just his kindness because he could see that she was all over the place.

She wanted him to touch her properly. She wanted him to sweep her into his arms, to kiss her, hold her close and whisper heaven only knew what in her ear. Not sweet nothings, because she was sure that wasn't something he did.

Confused and out of her depth, Kaya tried to work out what it was, exactly, she wanted this man to do. Did she want the one thing she had always promised herself she would never want—sex for the sake of sex? For them to be two ships passing in the night with no love involved and no plans for a future? It was horrifying and scary to think that she could jettison her hard-held beliefs for someone who couldn't have been less appropriate.

Frankly, it beggared belief.

But she was still sitting still and she still hadn't asked him to move his hand, and when she did finally find her voice, she barely recognised it.

'We should go in. It's getting cold out here.'

'We should.'

'You're looking at me,' Kaya heard herself whisper and her heart skipped a beat when he smiled at her. It was the sort of smile she imagined he would deliver when he was with a woman and wasn't busy arguing with her. A slow, toe-curling, sexy smile that made the world stop turning.

'It's no hardship.'

Kaya had no idea what would have happened next if he hadn't been the first to pull back, to rake his fingers through his hair and then glance outside briefly, taking hold of a situation that had felt dangerously out of control.

She jerked back, all in a fluster. Her breath was rapid, as if she'd been running a marathon, and when she opened her mouth nothing emerged.

It was a relief when he let himself out of the

car, moving round to her side to open the door. Out here the snow was still thick and deep in the places where it hadn't been cleared.

The tyres had left skid marks through the snow like slanting exclamation marks where she had screeched to a stop, dark and muddy against the pristine white.

Kaya didn't notice any of this. She was just aware of the beating of her heart, the racing of her pulse and the guy opening the car door.

That would be why she lost her footing. Why else? She clambered out of her four-wheel drive, and didn't pay a scrap of attention to the deep furrow of snow banked up at the side. She didn't trip over anything, she just tumbled into a fall—an awkward, clumsy fall—and his lunge to catch her was as clumsy because of the impediment of the snow.

But catch her he did, and he swept her up in one easy movement.

For a millisecond, Kaya luxuriated in the feel of him, his hardness against her, the strength of his arms around her. A millisecond of stolen, treacherous pleasure.

'Put me down!'

'Just as soon as we're inside. Don't lock the car. I'll come back to fetch my computer.'

'I don't need you carrying me!'

'I don't need you stumbling to the front door and doing more damage to your ankle.'

'My ankle is just fine.'

'I'll give you my verdict once I've checked it over.'

'You are *the* most arrogant guy I've ever met in my entire life!'

'I know. Is that a bad thing?'

Kaya shivered, every bit of her body tingling in response to his proximity and to the husky teasing in his voice.

They were in the house, which was blessedly warm, and she gave up the fight and subsided into him as he headed to the sitting room and deposited her on the sofa, as gently as if she were a piece of priceless china.

Her instinct had been to repel the act of kindness. It was something she wasn't used to. She was tall, strong and accustomed to looking out for herself.

His sudden tenderness was disconcerting, as was his gentleness as he eased off her boot, followed by her thick, insulated socks. He was kneeling at her feet and she was absorbed in the moment as she watched his dark head. She had to resist the temptation to sift her fingers through his hair.

'Tell me if this hurts.'

'It hurts!'

'Sprain. Nothing serious. Is there a first-aid kit in the kitchen? Bathroom? You just need it to be contained with a compress and keep the weight off it for a day or two.'

'Suddenly you're a doctor? There's a first-aid kit in the kitchen. It's in the cupboard next to the sink.'

'I'm a man of many talents.' He glanced up at her, and their eyes met and remained locked long enough for Kaya to lick her lips as nervous tension ratcheted up a couple of notches.

She suddenly found that considerate and gentle Leo was a lot more difficult to handle than arrogant and infuriating Leo.

'Don't move a muscle. I'll be back in a minute.'

Move a muscle? Kaya felt as weak as a kitten as she watched him vanish. Her eyes drifted to the coat he'd dumped on one of the chairs in the sitting room and her mind drifted to the look in his eyes in the car, the huskiness of his voice when he'd told her that looking at her was no hardship...

She was doing a balancing act on uneven ground and...wow...quicksand had never felt so good.

She tensed when he re-entered the room less than a minute later, and her breath hitched in her throat as he began to wind the compress around her ankle. She'd never thought that big hands could be so delicate.

'Where did you learn how to do that?' she asked gruffly, to break the stifling silence.

There was a smile when he replied.

'Foster care wasn't all bad. There was a rota when you got to a certain age—first-aid cover. We had some basic training over a two-day period. Plenty of opportunity for kids of eleven to fool around with medical equipment and ask stupid questions. I can't imagine what the guy who came in to instruct us would have thought of all the horseplay—maybe he expected it. At any rate, he did a good job…and I can tell you that if you suddenly choke on a fish bone tonight, I should be able to see you through.'

'I can't picture you as a kid.'

Leo rested back on his haunches to look at her with a crooked smile. 'Sometimes, neither can I. You need to have a bath. I'm going to carry you upstairs and run a bath for you.'

'No, I'm fine!'

'Nonsense. You wouldn't make it up the stairs without a lot of discomfort. I've already broken the ice by bringing you into the house…'

Kaya nodded jerkily. Did she mind him carrying her up the stairs? No. She wanted him to. She wanted a repeat performance of her body melting surreptitiously against his while her mind took off in all sorts of forbidden directions.

She wanted to have time out from being careful.

There was no danger when it came to this guy because he wasn't her type. She might be madly attracted to him, but she could never really fall for someone who had a commitment-phobia, someone who probably enjoyed relationships that lasted five minutes and then disappeared. She was just too serious when it came to the heavy stuff.

But this wasn't heavy. This was superficial, illicit enjoyment, the sort of stuff her teenage self might have got up to if that teenage girl hadn't been so busy taking care of the person who should have been taking care of her.

'That's true. And I really do feel a bit grubby. If you wouldn't mind running a bath for me, then yes, that would be helpful.'

'Does this mean that you're not going to argue with me about it?'

'Why would I?'

'Because you're argumentative?'

'Weirdly, I'm not at all.' But she didn't want to return to the subject of *why* she was so argumentative when she was with him. She didn't want to get bogged down, yet again, in the business of trying to get him to understand her point of view. That ship had sailed. He'd made that patently clear and she would just have to deal with the fallout of his decision.

This brief truce between them felt too good to endanger. She reached for him as he leant to scoop her up and relaxed as he carried her up the stairs. She was five-ten, but he made her feel petite and light as a feather.

'I'll run a bath for you.' He stood back, having settled her on the comfy chair by the window. 'Try not to get the compress wet, but it might be tricky.'

'I'll manage,' Kaya told him gruffly. 'I can drape my leg over the side of the bath and it'll be no problem wriggling my way out. I'm pretty athletic.'

Leo grunted.

Did she have any idea what images she was generating in his head? He pictured her naked in the water, bubbles not quite covering her belly and her breasts... Her legs apart with one resting on the lip of the bath...

If he wasn't careful he'd be having a cold shower at roughly the same time as she was having her hot bath.

Leo had never been turned on by pursuit of the inaccessible. He had built his life around work with everything falling into place around it. And that included the relationships he had.

They came and went and they never interfered with his work. When it came to pursuit, he was really only interested in the kind that involved the acquisition of power and money. Neither was essential, per se, but having lived his life deprived of both they certainly held quite a bit of appeal.

Certainly for him.

As far as he was concerned, time involved chasing a woman made no sense. Bed was the final destination and sooner or later boredom was the eventual outcome. So why waste time on courtship?

Maybe he was lazy when it came to the opposite sex. Maybe all his considerable energies were held in reserve for his primary focus. That was something Leo didn't dwell on.

What surprised him was just how much air time he was giving Kaya, a woman he had only just met. More than that, she was definitely inaccessible, yet he couldn't stop himself from wanting her. What was that all about?

He finished running the bath and then backed out, leaving her to her own devices, muttering something about preparing food for her.

Watching him edge hurriedly out of the bedroom, making sure to shut the door behind him, Kaya wondered whether he could be more obvious in his sudden desire to be rid of her company.

She debated whether to lock the bedroom door but why? She didn't know. He wasn't going to barge in on a tide of lust, that was for sure.

The bath was perfect. He'd managed to get the temperature just right and she took her time getting all her clothes off, manoeuvring slowly to avoid jarring her ankle, which felt better with the compress.

When she was naked, she stood, balancing on one foot, and looked at her own nakedness in the mirror. It wasn't something she usually did. What she saw was a tall and slender woman with small, high breasts and a neat waist. A strong, toned body.

When she examined herself through a guy's eyes, though, the picture was different. Too tall…too flat-chested…too boyish and athletic. Did men like strong women? At a push she could probably lift up a lot of the guys she knew. Was that sexy?

She took her time in the bath because she was thinking, while the time passed by. Thinking about Leo and this curling desire inside her that was so alien, so exciting and so difficult to deal with.

She feverishly turned over in her head the way he had backed out of the bathroom earlier, as though the hounds of hell had been snapping at his heels.

In her mind, she played over every word spoken that evening, every look exchanged, and wondered whether she was reading meaning into things that had been insignificant.

She cursed her own inexperience, which was crazy, because there was no way she could go back in time and adjust her life to fit this one moment.

What shocked and unsettled her too was the fact that Julie Anne and the huge secret she had kept to herself, which had preyed on her mind for all the time she'd been in New Zealand, had somehow ended up taking second place to Leo. How could that be? She was terrified to think that she could be like her mother—drawn to a rich guy who knew how to talk the talk and walk the walk but would always be as unreliable as the day was long.

She *needed* reliability. It was part of her emotional foundations.

Only when the water was getting tepid did Kaya realise just how long she'd been in the bath. She made to move and winced as her ankle took the brunt of her weight as she levered herself up.

The water sloshed around her as she gripped the sides of the bath. Every ounce of effort was focused on the time-consuming business of getting out and protecting her sore ankle at the same time, and the chill of the air on her skin was bringing her out in goose pimples.

She didn't hear the soft push of the bathroom door. She was frowning and concentrating hard, and it was only when she glanced across that she saw Leo's hand on the door, his shadow on the tiled floor.

'You okay in there?'

Kaya's head went blank. She felt heat pour through her body, and she knew she should say something, but her vocal cords had seized up and all she could manage was an inaudible croak.

And then the door was pushed open and there he was, the guy she'd spent the last forty minutes thinking about while the bath water had gone cold, her skin had puckered and he...*what*?

He'd left her to have a bath and she'd taken so long that he'd understandably become worried—just as she'd understandably been worried when he'd headed into town on foot in the snow...

'Leo!'

'Kaya...'

They spoke at the same time.

'Get out!'

The words seemed to hit Leo from a long way away. He'd done his best to clear his head in the kitchen, and had taken his time making them both something to eat. But when he'd glanced at the clock on the wall, and seen just how long it had been since he'd run that bath, he'd felt a little tendril of worry begin to curl inside him.

He'd left the food in the kitchen and headed up the stairs, and then he'd listened by the door and heard nothing. He'd knocked softly and then increasingly harder but had heard nothing. And then, with his hand on the bathroom door, he'd heard something that had sounded very much like a cry of pain and gut instinct had taken over.

He stared.

Her body… How long had he been fantasising about her body without realising it? How long had he been telling himself that this woman was out of bounds? That whatever attraction he felt was rooted in nothing more than the kick of novelty and the strangeness of the bond between them in the form of his mother?

She was beyond beautiful. Her body was a golden olive. Her glaring eyes were bright and dark and her long, soaking wet hair streamed over her body, clinging to her shoulders and falling in strands to partially cover small, perfect breasts.

She was supporting herself on the bath. He could see the strain of sinew in her arms, and beyond that the length of slender legs and the dark thatch between them.

Their eyes met, she yelled at him again and the spell was broken. Leo reddened, averting his eyes as he backed away.

For the first time in his life he was in a situation over which he had absolutely no control. She was the most glorious thing he had ever seen in his life, and he could have stayed looking at her until the sun rose in the sky. But instead, perspiring, flustered and slamming the bathroom door shut behind him, he fled.

CHAPTER FIVE

KAYA COULDN'T HIDE in the bedroom for ever, but she wished she could. She was on fire as she got dressed. When she thought of Leo bursting in on her, seeing her naked, her thoughts went into meltdown and she wanted the ground to open up and swallow her whole.

Mortification, blind fury, horrifying self-consciousness: she honestly didn't know which was the strongest emotion. What had gone through his head when he had seen her? She tried to recapture what she'd seen on his face and the only thing she could come up with was…shock.

But then what had he expected when he'd decided to waltz into her bedroom uninvited and then, to top it off, enter the bathroom, knowing that she would be in it?

She looked at her reflection in the mirror and what stared back at her was a woman whose colour was so high and whose eyes were glittering so brightly that she seemed on the point of combusting. She had thrown on her jeans and several layers and had managed to put on socks, even though her ankle was still sore and tender. With her emotions running high, though, it was very easy to overlook her twisted ankle.

She made it very slowly down the stairs, clutching the banister, and with each passing step her fury increased. By the time she finally made it to the kitchen, she was bolstered by self-righteous anger, which had the great advantage of diminishing her excoriating embarrassment.

She pushed open the kitchen door and the first thing she saw was Leo at the kitchen table. He looked up as soon as she entered.

His computer was open on the table—the Wi-Fi had been restored at some point during the day—but she could tell that he hadn't been working. His eyes were brooding, intense, and she noted the dark flush that spread across his sharp cheekbones as their gaze held and kept holding for what seemed like an eternity.

'How *dare* you?'

Fired up, Kaya hobbled into the kitchen and, when he half-rose to help her to a chair, she glared at him.

'Kaya, I'm sorry if I busted in on you while you were—'

'Don't even say it!'

The last thing she needed was to be reminded

of her nudity when he had barged into the bath-room unannounced.

She was burning up. How could he sit there, as cool as a cucumber, while she was *burning up*? And how could her body be so *aware* of him even though her head was fuming, hating him and going over what had happened in those brief *seconds* in torturous detail?

Her brain was being sensible and giving her the ammunition to rage, but her body…that was a different matter. She thought of his eyes rest-ing on her, *seeing* her the way no man had ever seen her before, and something tingled between her thighs and made her nipples tighten in crazy awareness, filled her veins with a rush of hot blood.

And her disobedient eyes were trying hard to put him into perspective, to see him as the stranger who had turned her world upside down by inconsiderately showing up before she'd had time to get her house in order. But instead all she could see was his ridiculously handsome face: the sharp, chiselled features, the thick, sooty lashes and those deep, dark eyes watch-ing her without revealing anything.

'I knocked.'

'That's a lie!'

'Let me get you something to eat…to drink.'

'I'm not hungry!'

'Kaya...'

'You might own this house but that doesn't mean that you can open and shut doors without knocking first.'

'I knocked!' He vaulted to his feet, pausing briefly to stand in front of her and meet her furious eyes head on.

In his head, he saw her naked coming out of that bath, water streaming over her beautiful, supple body. He couldn't get the image out of his mind, and when he next spoke his voice was low and hoarse.

'I knocked, Kaya. I was worried. I left you alone and came down here, and the minutes ticked by, and the next time I looked at the clock nearly an hour had gone by and, damn it, I was worried!'

He stared at her, raked his fingers through his hair and was overwhelmed. Overwhelmed, now that he was verbalising how he'd felt, by astonishment at just how worried he had been that something had happened to her—that she'd fallen, banged her head, knocked herself out, hell, pretty much gone and done anything to herself.

She wasn't his responsibility!

So why had he been worried sick about her?

Worrying sick about anybody just wasn't in his DNA. He didn't have that gene. He knew what strength and independence felt like and they didn't include vivid scenarios in his head that bore no relation to reality when he sat down and analysed them.

He was way too emotionally detached for any show of weakness along those lines. He wondered whether, in some weird low-level way, he *did* feel responsible for her and decided that, if he did, then it made perfect sense. She was in his house, temporarily displaced because of him, and while she was there then surely he couldn't treat her with the sort of bone-deep detachment with which he treated everybody else?

And then...there was the connection to his mother, the woman he had never known. Kaya had known her. It was a peculiar situation. When he'd arrived here, the last thing he'd expected to find, or perhaps the last thing he'd had any interest in finding, had been connections to the woman who had given him up for adoption.

Yet, he had not been able to escape the slow build-up of a picture he hadn't asked to see. The mere fact that Kaya was who she was, and there was no denying her inherent *goodness*, gave him the sort of insight into the woman who had given birth to him that he hadn't asked for

However hard he subconsciously tried to prevent his thoughts from meandering into areas he knew would always prove futile, he still found himself doing it. He told her that her pleas for him to try and see Julie Anne for the person she had been before she had died were falling on deaf ears, and *of course* they were, but even so...

His imagination had been stirred, much to his annoyance. So it was a complex situation—little wonder his responses weren't in line with what he would have expected them to be!

'I don't need you being worried on my behalf,' Kaya snapped.

'You could have fallen...hurt yourself.'

'And I definitely *don't* need a knight in shining armour to rescue me from an accident that never happened!'

'Trust me,' Leo ground out, 'No one on this planet would ever be tempted to call me a knight in shining armour...'

Their eyes tangled. He moved towards her and pulled a chair so close to her he could see the luminous, satiny smoothness of her skin close up.

'I'll bet,' Kaya returned in a driven undertone, but her heart was beating fast and there was a swooping inside her that made her mouth go dry.

He might not be a knight in shining armour but he had taken care of her after she'd twisted her ankle. It had been a simple accident but she knew that there were guys who, in a similar position, would have seen her as a nuisance, hobbling around and taking up space in a house they had come to sell.

She thought of him carrying her up those stairs, thought of the gentle way he had examined her ankle and the way he had done his utmost to make sure she was relaxed because of how highly strung and sensitive she'd been with him, and she felt a whoosh of shame at her ungracious attack on him now.

He wouldn't have just barged in for the hell of it.

He just wasn't that sort of guy.

'I—I,' she stuttered, blushing. 'I apologise if I sound a little harsh. I guess I didn't hear you knocking. But you didn't knock on the bathroom door. You just pushed it open and stormed inside!'

'I pushed it open because I heard something that sounded like a grunt of pain.'

'I was trying to get out of the bath.' The water had gone cold, which showed just how long she'd been in it. Was it so surprising that he'd wondered what the hell had happened to her?

'I didn't stop to think, Kaya, and I should have—but what if something had happened to you? What if you were lying on the ground in pain?'

Kaya had an uncomfortable image of herself on the tiles in nothing but her birthday suit, being discovered by Leo and carried to the bed, exposed in all her glory.

She blanched at the vividness of the picture in her head and then breathed in sharply as their eyes met. She felt exposed, as if he could read her mind.

'I may have overreacted,' she said stiffly. 'It was the shock, I suppose, of having you…someone, anyone… I didn't expect it. You caught me…'

'I know how I caught you.'

Leo wanted to groan aloud. Did she have any idea what this conversation was doing to his head, never mind his body?

He couldn't help himself. His eyes flickered over her, from her beautiful face to the shape of her under the layers of clothes. In his mind's eye, he could still see those small, high breasts, the brown discs of her nipples, the curve of her spine, the slenderness of her ankles and the dark shadow of her pubic hair…

His breathing slowed and his eyes darkened.

'You're beautiful, Kaya,' he heard himself say, his voice low and husky, and he sat back and pressed his thumbs to his eyes. 'God, I have no idea what possessed me to say that and I apologise.'

He leapt up, prowled through the kitchen, restless in his own body, and then returned to the kitchen table. But he pulled the chair back, close enough so he wouldn't have to shout but not so close that his nervous system would begin misbehaving.

'I've made you feel uncomfortable and for that I can't apologise enough. I…' He sighed, half-closed his eyes and flung his head back for a few seconds, a man in the grip of something strong and elemental. 'I'm going to leave you… head to one of the other rooms to work. Internet's back on. Kaya, I would offer to carry you upstairs, but I'm guessing you'd probably tell me to get lost.'

'I can make my own way up.'

Had he just told her that she was beautiful? It had sounded like a confession ripped from him, and the sincerity of it had gone to the very core of her and opened the lid of a box she'd been struggling to keep tightly locked. It was a box that contained wild ideas and reckless yearnings…things she'd only seen and felt since this man had appeared on the scene.

This was the very thing she had always sworn she would never do. She'd noted the example her mother had set and made a pact with herself that she would never let some guy rule her head, never mind her heart. She would steer clear of the temptation to let anyone dominate her thoughts. She was never going to be the woman sitting by the phone, biting her nails and desperately waiting for it to ring.

She wanted him to carry her up. She wanted to feel his hardness against her. She wanted him to carry on telling her stuff she knew was out of bounds. She wanted to hear him say more—that he fancied her, that he wanted to touch her, kiss her…*make love to her.*

'Look at me like that,' Leo warned in a driven undertone, 'And you might get a little more than you bargained for.'

'Like what?'

'Right now, I want to kiss you so much it's a physical pain. More than just kiss you, Kaya.'

'What? What more?'

'I'm going to go. This is…'

'C-crazy,' she confirmed shakily.

'So you feel it too.'

'It doesn't matter what I feel. Nothing…nothing…is going to happen. It would be madness. I… I could never… You don't make sense, not to me. Not for someone like me.' And she meant it. She didn't understand how this powerful thing had ignited between them—how it had ignited inside *her*, as though she'd just been a bundle of dry tinder waiting for the wrong guy to come along one day with a box of matches to set her alight—but it had.

Which didn't mean she would do anything about it. No way. She wasn't her mother. She wasn't going to get lost in some bad-news guy. She had her head screwed on even if, right now, her body was doing its best to dictate the state of play.

'I get it,' Leo returned roughly.

He looked away but he could feel her eyes on him and he was held captive by something he couldn't identify, something that was doing a damn good job of making him lose all his legendary cool.

Somehow he'd turned into a horny teenager and all he wanted to do was reach out and touch her. The fact that she wanted him just as much as he wanted her was almost too much to take on board. How the hell were they going to make it under the same roof for another day, hour, minute?

'It's late. Sure you don't want me to help you up?' He spread his hands in a gesture of appeasement. 'You have my word that, however much I'm attracted to you, there's no way you need fear that I'll make a play for you. Not now, not while we're under the same roof. You have my word.'

Kaya believed him with every fibre in her

being. She told him she was tired, would grab a couple of tablets for the discomfort and make herself a sandwich. That she was fine.

What she wanted to say was *what if she wanted him to make a play for her? What if she wanted this mutual attraction to take them wherever it wanted to take them...?*

'I don't think we should talk about this again.' She cleared her throat and assumed a firm line, drawing a marker in the sand. Because who knew what was going to happen without that marker? And, whatever this was, she intended to fight it. So would he. They were both adults, and she might be inexperienced, but she wasn't a complete idiot.

'Are you saying we pretend this never happened?'

'That's not impossible.'

'No,' Leo said softly. 'It's not.'

And it was exactly what should happen. She was as fresh as dew on a summer's morning. Her world had been turned upside down, so add *vulnerable* on top of everything else. Whatever this crazy force was running between them, he knew that it was up to him to stamp all over it.

But he hesitated. Those eyes, those softly parted lips... His mind was running amok with forbidden images. He could feel the steel of his erection throbbing painfully and the ache of a need he'd never thought possible.

The silence sizzled between them, an electric charge that could deliver a shock Leo knew both of them would regret. He, because he didn't do complicated situations and this turned *complicated* into an understatement. And she, because who knew where that door would lead to if she decided to dump the principles that had guided her life? One of them had to lead by experience, and that was going to be him, whether he liked it or not.

Because one look at those softly parted lips, and the barely concealed desire darkening her eyes, and he knew that whatever caresses he gave her would be returned in full.

But would there be regrets after? Probably. He didn't do post-coital regrets.

'Let me bring you the tablets, Kaya. They'll kick in fast and make it easier for you to move about.'

He didn't give her a choice. He had to escape the drag of wanting something that would do him no good, would do neither of them any good.

He fetched tablets and water for her and had to control a crazy tremor in his hands as he dropped them on the table, before standing back and folding his arms.

'I'll see you in the morning.'

'I'll start my packing. I know you're not going to chuck me out, but the sooner things are finalised here, the better.'

Leo shrugged and left, shutting the door quietly behind him, and it was only when she was alone in the kitchen that Kaya sagged into the chair and closed her eyes.

It wouldn't be mentioned—none of it. That was the thought she hugged to herself an hour and a half later when she finally made it up to bed.

As he had predicted, the painkillers had done their job and the pain in her ankle had subsided to a dull throb by the time she was under the covers with the bedroom door firmly locked, although she knew that the last thing he would do would be enter without being invited.

The air had been cleared between them. That was a good thing. There had been a dark cloud, heavy with things unsaid, thick with innuendo and slanted, glancing, shivering awareness. She'd thought that she was the only one feeling it, but she hadn't been, and she told herself that there was no harm in secretly admitting that his attraction to her made her feel euphoric and heady.

The guy was sex on legs. What woman

wouldn't be flattered to have his attention turned to her?

If this *thing* between them hadn't gone by the time morning came, then surely the fact that they had agreed to pretend nothing had been said would help things along?

And anyway, she thought, coming back down to earth with a bump as sleep finally began to take over, whatever passing attraction he felt for her would be one that had grown from their proximity and from the fact that they were connected by Julie Anne, whether he wanted to admit it or not.

He was an experienced guy, unlike her, and she was sure that, having been turned away, his attitude would be a mental shrug and a 'you win a few, you lose a few' response.

Sleep eventually came but it was fitful. Her ankle felt better but, in the dead of the night, she blamed it for keeping her awake, even though deep down she knew that the thing keeping her alert and aware was happening in her head.

She wasn't sure what she'd hoped the morning would bring when she went downstairs, but she was on the defensive the second she found him in the kitchen.

If she had appreciated his stunning looks before, nothing could have prepared her for how devastatingly aware she was of him now that they had opened up about their mutual attraction. Just knowing that he found her attractive added an edge to their situation that brought her out in a cold sweat.

His eyes rested on her, dark and brooding, but when he spoke it was to ask her how her ankle was doing.

She'd told him that it would be best for them to pretend that nothing had happened and he was going along with that. It was obvious in his politeness and in the cool remoteness of his expression. He was going to be considerate and courteous until they parted company.

'I've decided that I'm going to head out today,' she said, keeping as cool as he was. She hadn't thought about going out, and had planned to spend the day clearing more of her stuff, but suddenly the thought of them both circling one another in the house and pretending nothing had happened was too much.

'You're heading out?'

Kaya bristled.

Wherever she looked, he seemed to fill her vision. She had surprised him as he was making himself a cup of coffee and, even though he was in some faded track bottoms and an old sweatshirt, he still managed to look unfairly sexy.

She harked back to him telling her that he found her attractive, to the hot urgency of their conversation the evening before, and instantly felt like passing out.

'It's not a crime, is it?' She blushed because she didn't want to sound defensive. 'Snow's clearing up,' she said abruptly. 'I thought I might take the opportunity to head into town, visit the halfway house. I haven't been there for over two months and I miss it.'

'The halfway house…?'

'Yes.'

'Not a good idea.'

'Why not? I was fine driving yesterday when the weather was worse. I'm accustomed to conditions out here.'

'And I'm accustomed to pounding the pavements of Manhattan in winter, but I'd draw the line at doing that with a twisted ankle.'

'My ankle is better.'

'Really? And what if it decides otherwise while you're behind the wheel of your car? Never mind the fact that you could get into an accident and hurt yourself, you could also get into an accident and hurt other people.'

Kaya shot him a fulminating look from under her lashes.

'Well,' she said sweetly, changing tack and taking advantage of the opportunity suddenly provided to her, 'You could always come with me.'

'Why would I want to do that?'

Caught up in the moment of playing it cool and banking down a libido that had suddenly awakened the second she had entered the kitchen, Leo stilled. Hadn't they parked conversations about the inheritance he hadn't asked for? Every time he thought about it—which was too often for his liking—his head was flooded with all sorts of questions.

What had the woman been like? Over time, all thoughts he had had of her—of which none, thankfully, had continued to intrude until now—had solidified into an image of a woman happy to put herself above everything and everyone. Someone grasping, selfish and unpleasant. Those were impressions he had never had any trouble dealing with.

But, now that he was here, he hated the fact that those impressions had become out of focus. Kaya had clearly loved the woman, and certainly it would seem that she had done many things that were commendable, if Kaya was to be believed.

So who had she been?

Leo loathed the curiosity that kept raising its head because he knew the question about *why* she had dumped him would remain a mystery, whatever had happened thereafter.

And underneath that corrosive curiosity was the simple, jarring hurt of knowing that the love that he had missed out on had been lavished on Kaya. He didn't resent that but it was still something else he found himself dealing with.

The last thing he needed was Kaya taking a few more pot shots at him, although grudgingly he had to commend her for her tenacity, if nothing else.

But, then again, wasn't that one of the things that made her so appealing—the strength he sensed underneath the innocence? He guessed she could be as stubborn as a mule, and outspoken with it, and those were qualities in short supply when it came to the women he had always dated. He frowned impatiently but without much surprise when she continued, with gathering momentum.

'Because if you're that concerned about me making it there in one piece without laying waste to myself, not to mention everyone in my path when my ankle suddenly decides to hit the accelerator by accident, then you don't have an option. You come with me and take the wheel, or I go on my own.'

It was a bluff. She hadn't thought about what might happen if her foot did slip. There was no way she would endanger anyone by doing anything irresponsible, but this seemed a great way of forcing his hand.

What was the worst that could happen? He

could refuse, yell at her, tell her to mind her own business. He could storm out of the kitchen in a rage because she'd pulled the dragon's tail.

She realised that anything would be better than the polite treatment he had been giving her. Having laid down ground rules, she was now discovering that she didn't much like them being adhered to.

He was being the perfect gentleman and she didn't want a perfect gentleman. Whatever he had released, whatever temptation he had dangled in front of her, she now had a taste for it. She liked the thrill of seduction.

She'd never felt anything like it and she wondered whether this was what her mother had felt time and time again. But no… When Kaya took a step back and looked at this situation rationally, she knew that it was nothing like what her mother had succumbed to over and over. This wasn't a reckless search for love, clinging to crumbs thrown at her, desperate for the comfort of settling down and finding stability.

She wasn't her mother.

She knew the score even though she wasn't experienced when it came to sex. She knew what to avoid and she knew that, when it came to anything long-term, Leo was definitely not made of the right material.

When she thought like that, she felt a disturbing sliver of excitement race through her.

Who needed the right material all the time? Had that been a mistake—to put all her eggs in one basket? To think that, if she couldn't have it all—the complete fairy-tale, happy-ever-after ending—then it was better to have nothing at all?

He was looking at her in guarded silence and Kaya side-stepped all those unsettling thoughts. She couldn't afford to go there. Could she?

'It's up to you,' she said with a casual shrug, rising to her feet and then over-egging the pudding by wincing, a reminder that the sore ankle—which actually felt as good as new—could hive off at any given moment while she was driving and do its own thing.

'You win.' Leo growled, standing up to glare at her. 'Give me ten minutes. And in case you're wondering…' He reached to where she kept her car keys on a hook by the kitchen door and slipped them into his pocket with a grin. 'We'll take my car.'

CHAPTER SIX

'HOW DID YOU get involved with this place? Now that we're heading there, you might just as well fill me in.'

Leo slanted a sideways glance at the woman sitting next to him, staring through the window with just the smallest of smiles on her face.

He fancied he could detect triumph there. There was no point agitating for an argument about this trip to a place he had no interest in seeing. Truth was, her ankle appeared to be fine, judging from her easy walk to the car. She'd made a show of limping around the kitchen but had obviously forgotten to prolong the act once she'd managed to get him on board for a visit to the halfway house.

'Where to start?' Kaya murmured.

'Perhaps not at the very beginning,' Leo suggested politely. 'A brief summing up might be the best idea.'

Kaya glanced across. She'd felt his eyes on

her but now he was staring straight ahead, concentrating on the road. Although the snow had stopped falling, there was still sufficient banked to the side to make driving conditions hazardous.

It was a beautiful morning: bright-blue skies and everything in sharp relief, from the silhouettes of the wintry trees with their naked branches to the crisp colours of the occasional farm house they passed, burrowed far from the road, just about visible across snow-covered fields.

Cities might hold the buzz of excitement but nothing could really beat the peace of a place like this, where people had time to appreciate the small details that nature gave them, from the grass growing in summer, to the leaves falling in autumn and the wondrous vastness of the open, uncluttered skies.

'I'll try but the beginning is a long time ago, when my mother first moved here from Alaska. I know you don't want to talk about Julie Anne…'

'Don't worry yourself about me. Trust me, my sensibilities are remarkably resilient. A few facts and figures might prepare me for what I'm going to find, so you can stick to that brief.'

Kaya had no intention of throwing him a few facts and figures or sticking to any such brief. She had a suspicion as to what he meant by 'sticking to the facts and figures'. A profit-and-loss column so that he could work out how much he could get for the place when the time came for him to fire-sell it, along with everything else.

Hadn't she already tried to appeal to his better nature? Sexy as hell he might be, but when it came to the properties that were now his, the very properties he had ordered her not to bother talking about, any sign of a better nature was not in evidence.

It would take them the better part of forty-five minutes to get to the halfway house. On a clear day and a good run, it could be done in half that time from the house, but the going was slow in these conditions. She had every intention of laying it on thick, because this would be her one and only chance to have her say.

'Julie Anne wasn't living in the town when my mother lived here. I know that because she told me when we headed south from Alaska. A lot of her friends had left the place but some had stayed, had kids. My mum found out fast enough that Julie Anne had become something of a pillar of the community when she moved here.'

'A pillar of the community. Touching.'

Kaya didn't say anything but she could see

from the clench of his jaw and the narrowing of his mouth that this was painful, and her heart went out to him. He was as tough as steel but underneath that armour there was more. She knew it. She'd seen it in the way he had been so gentle with her when she'd twisted her ankle.

His reaction gave her hope that maybe all wasn't lost, at least not as lost as she'd thought.

'My mum made friends with her quickly. We had a tiny little rented place in the centre above a shop. Julie Anne used to come to the shop quite a bit to buy stuff for the halfway house, odd bits and pieces. She and mum struck up a friendship of sorts. They reached an arrangement—I'm not sure how that came about but my mum…could be very persuasive. I ended up getting a babysitter without mum having to shell out. She could do her job and have her fun and there would be back-up when she wasn't around.'

'Very persuasive indeed. Is that why you go out of your way to be the opposite?'

But Kaya heard the teasing smile in his voice and, instead of bristling with offence, she felt a rush of warmth that made her skin prickle. She relaxed into her narrative. She'd never been this open before when it came to revealing her thoughts. She retraced her childhood, took side turns to describe stuff she'd kept to herself and built up a picture of the woman who had become so influential in her life.

Leo listened. In many ways, her childhood had been as tough as his. From everything she said, it seemed she'd skipped the business of having fun and had gone straight into the hard work of looking out for a mother who had been young, irresponsible and scattered when it came to men. She went for the wrong kind... She involved her daughter in the ups and downs of an erratic love life... She'd lost her husband, who had been the great love of her life, and had then proceeded to throw herself into years of futile distraction tactics in a vain attempt to replace him.

He'd gleaned the basics of her story before but, as they drove slowly towards the halfway house, those basics became fleshed out, building a picture of a girl who had been forced to grow up way before her time.

'So that's pretty much what's leading me to my involvement with the halfway house.' Kaya blushed.

'Ah, we get there at last.'

'You're laughing at me.'

'I enjoyed the story-telling.' He glanced across to her and, for a couple of seconds, his dark eyes remained fixed on her pink cheeks. 'And I'm not laughing at you. I had gathered things were difficult for you growing up, but the picture you paint fills in all the blank spaces. You must have been overjoyed when your mother met the guy who eventually became your stepfather.'

'I was,' Kaya admitted. 'I didn't see it coming and it took a while. My mother had become so accustomed to falling for the wrong guy that when the right guy made it on the scene she didn't see him at first for the great person he was.' She smiled. 'She got the ending she wanted. It just took a while and a lot of wrong turns to get there.'

Leo didn't say anything. Was this the girl who believed that love stories really did come true? An alarm bell sounded, a distant one. One that made him say, thoughtfully, 'I suppose that's a road that plays out for some people—the wrong turns and the happy ending.'

'But not for you?'

'Never for me.'

Well, if she were to be silly enough to entertain any ideas about a proper relationship with this guy, then he'd as good as told her not to bother. Had he been warning her off him? Or had that just been a natural response to what she had said?

'Up ahead, around that bend—the halfway house is there. It's a little way out of the town. I think Julie Anne must have located it there so that none of the locals could lodge any complaints although, after all this time, they're very kindly disposed to the girls who come and go. Once a year, there's a fundraiser, and the proceeds go to maintenance of the place.'

Her thoughts were buzzing in her head as his flash car pulled into the courtyard outside the house. There were eight other cars parked in front, all in a neat row to the side where an attempt had been made to define some parking bays.

For a few seconds after she got out, Kaya stood by the side of the car and gazed at the building she hadn't been near in months. When she looked at Leo, it was to see him doing exactly the same thing, looking at it.

It was large, a large, grey square with evenly spaced windows, and surrounded by trees. In summer, it was striking. Now, in winter, it looked bleak and a little run-down.

Leo had moved to stand next to her and for a few seconds he took in the sight of the place his mother had founded, his saintly mother who had been a pillar of the community, doing so much for so many, having abandoned one.

His mouth thinned.

He'd long ago trained himself never to dwell on things that couldn't be changed, but now he could feel a groundswell of confusion and bitterness.

Next to him, Kaya resumed chatting, walking towards the house, her voice high and excited, her hands shoved into the pockets of her windcheater.

He followed. He was already regretting the impulse that had brought him here. He should have called her bluff with the ankle story, for there were no signs of any twisted ankle now. Instead, here he was, forced to accept that the woman who had given him up for adoption had managed to find it in herself to lavish her dedication on complete strangers.

And, once inside the house, nothing changed his mind. It was roomy and bustling, a mixture of offices, rooms for relaxing in, bedrooms and a kitchen that had been fashioned out of two spacious rooms knocked into one. The kitchen was big enough to sit at least a couple of dozen people at the extended pine table.

There were people everywhere. In one of the rooms, there was a table-tennis table, a cinema-sized television and pockets of deep, comfortable chairs in which young women, most either pregnant or holding tiny babies, were sitting and chatting.

Everyone knew Kaya.

From behind her, Leo watched.

She introduced him to several of the employees but she was completely absorbed in the place, laughing, chatting and glancing into rooms.

With every passing step, Leo was reminded of the life his mother had managed to build in the aftermath of walking away from him. He couldn't wait to leave and yet...he could see the details of a life Kaya didn't want to see erased.

It was shortly before one by the time they were heading back to the house and for a few moments, as he manoeuvred out of the courtyard and away from the halfway house, there was silence.

Leo expected that she was thinking about where they'd been. It was obvious that everyone there absolutely adored her. They had flocked around her and she had been in her element, her interest and delight shining in her eyes and in her responses.

He picked up speed. There was no need for her to give him directions. He knew the way back.

'The place is falling apart at the seams,' he snapped into the silence and didn't look at her, although her lack of response said it all.

'Is that all you noticed?'

The sudden tension in her voice relaxed him. Why, he didn't know.

'I'm trained to notice details like that, especially in places I happen to own.'

Kaya forced herself to count to ten and to squash the tide of disappointment flooding her. 'Aside from that, what did you think?'

'What do you want me to say to that?'

'I want you to say that you were...impressed by what you found! I want you to say that you looked at all those young women, looked at the advantages the place has given them, and liked what you saw!'

Leo gritted his teeth, took a corner a little too sharply and slowed for a bit, but then picked up speed, heading back to the house with his emotions all over the place.

Silence seemed the best option when it came to getting his self-control back on track. Yet that very silence made him feel exposed and vulnerable, allowing insight into emotions he didn't want to put on display yet found impossible to keep concealed.

'Surely you can see that?'

'That *what*, Kaya?'

'You can see the woman Julie Anne was? She devoted her life to that place. Knew and took an interest in all the girls personally.'

'I'm sure she did.'

'So...'

'The place needs a whole lot of money pouring into it, Kaya. I'm guessing that, in between the fun and the laughter and the caring and the sharing, no one has taken the time to make a note of the beams that have woodworm, or the cracks in the ceiling, or the suspicious signs of damp in the kitchen?'

They were back at the house in record time. If the trip out had taken forty minutes at a leisurely pace, the trip back had taken half the time.

Leo leapt from the driver's seat at the same time as Kaya jumped out from her side, making sure to land on one foot, protecting her ankle just in case.

'Yes, everyone knows that there's work to be done on the place, Leo!' She wanted to reach out and hold him, but her hand dropped to her side before she could rest it on his arm. She watched as he inserted the key and noted how he fumbled for a bit before pushing open the door and standing back to allow her past him.

He spun round to look at her, raked his fingers through his hair and then stripped off his jacket, watching as she did the same, following him in getting rid of the layers, including the winter boots.

They stood facing one another.

'I didn't come here to pour money into one of Julie Anne's schemes,' he said in a driven un-

dertone. 'Have you any idea how much it would
cost to salvage that place before it starts col-
lapsing?'

'There were plans...costings done...before
Julie Anne died.'

'And you're trying to persuade me that I
should pick up the slack?' He shrugged but there
was a sour taste in his mouth, a feeling of loss
that made him angry and belligerent. 'As the
good Samaritan I've never been? I don't believe
the woman was much of a Samaritan thirty-odd
years ago, do you?'

'Leo, I'm sorry.'

Kaya's voice was low and quiet. She had ma-
nipulated him in visiting the shelter, and now
was torn apart by the notion that she might have
done the wrong thing, might have opened up
wounds that had been better left alone.

'She tried to atone, you know? That's what I
truly believe. I don't know why...why she did
what she did all that time ago. I don't have answers any more than you do, but why not judge
her on what happened next in her story?'

Leo stared at her, at her beautiful, open face
pleading with him to find a heart where there
was none.

Although, he'd seen the good the woman had
done, had been moved by what he had seen.

At odds with himself, restless in his own

skin, all he could see was Kaya in front of him. Her delicate floral scent filled his nostrils. He scowled, moved closer and groaned as he pulled her towards him. He couldn't resist and he didn't understand why. There was a lot he felt he didn't understand at that moment.

'What is this thing you do to me?' he whispered huskily. He detached, breathing in deeply. He was about to apologise and turn away, thoroughly ashamed that he hadn't been able to fight an urge that was bigger than him, but she pulled him back, drew him down and kissed him.

Leo held her and kissed her back, sliding his tongue into her mouth, meshing it against hers, barely able to contain his desire.

Kaya's lips parted and her eyes were heavy. So were her limbs, all of her heavy as lead, as if suddenly she could only move in slow motion, yet inside was fizzing with excitement.

'Are you sure about this?' Leo groaned against her mouth.

'I'm sure,' Kaya replied, her voice husky with desire. 'I've wanted this. You do things to me too, and I don't understand.'

'Upstairs, Kaya, or else it'll have to be right here.'

Kaya stood shakily and he swept her off her feet and carried her, moving fast, breathing hard. They got to the top of the stairs and he stopped, leant against the wall and swivelled her so that she was straddling him, and he kissed her, long, hard and urgently. Her fingers were wild in his hair, pulling him into her as close as he could get, so that there wasn't even an inch between them. She was shaking when they broke contact, and he was as well, shaking and barely holding on to control.

He pushed himself from the wall, still holding her.

She knew the house inside out, of course, but it still felt strange to be in his bedroom and to find herself in his bed.

Her head swam with images of them together on it, a swirling kaleidoscope of bodies moving as one, hot, sweaty and coming together.

Sex. The thing she'd always linked to *love*, the thing that had no place in her life unless there was affection, commitment, a future planned... All this time waiting, dreaming her dreams and making her plans, and here she was—sex was all she could think about, all she *wanted*.

Without making any conscious decision, Kaya knew that she wasn't going to breathe a word about her virginity. He'd run a mile if he knew that he was her first and the last thing she wanted this big, powerful man to do was run a mile.

He switched on the lamp by the bed and it cast a mellow glow through the room.

'I want to see you,' he said with a low, husky, shaky growl. 'You don't seem to have any idea how beautiful you are.'

He began undressing and she stared. The body underneath the clothing was so much more spectacular than all her fantasies put together: lean, muscular; he was the alpha male at the very peak of physical fitness. Even in the dim light she could make out the ripple of muscle and the tautness of his sinewy arms. He flung his clothes as he shed them on the ground, only extracting his wallet, which he dumped on the table by the bed.

'You're staring and I like it. Although not as much as I'd like to see you without anything on. But no, wait—allow me…'

Kaya swallowed hard as the reality of her inexperience hit her full-on. Any man who didn't do commitment and warned women not to expect anything from him was not a man who would jump for joy at the prospect of sleeping with a virgin.

She swept aside that momentary thought and abandoned herself to the glide of his hands as he sank onto the mattress with her. He was still in his boxers but she could see the impressive bulge of his erection. His fingers on her bare skin as he began easing clothes off her had her gritting her teeth for fear of crying out loud with pleasure.

With erotic mastery, he nuzzled her thighs, his tongue licking while his teeth grazed the tender, sensitive skin. She was still wearing her cotton undies and he delicately eased the crotch to one side so that he could burrow into the soft down between her legs.

Kaya sank into the caress with a guttural moan of pure pleasure and weaved her fingers into his hair at the same time, parting her legs so that he could deepen his gentle touch.

He did. He pushed his hands, stretching the underwear under them and pulled it off her.

Cool air hit her but she felt as if she was on fire.

Fierce desire devoured her. Her breathing was rapid and thick and she could barely think straight. How could she, when this man was making her feel things she'd never dreamed possible? How could something that had nothing to do with love feel so good?

She let herself get swept along on a tide of passion. She arched back as he followed the contours of her long, slender body with his tongue, from the delicate hollow of her belly button to the soft outline of her ribs, until that devastating trail ended with her breasts, with her nipples.

Somewhere along the line she had kicked off the underwear and ditched her bra, but she wasn't quite sure when, because she was in a hot daze.

'Please,' she begged. Her eyes were dark and drowsy when they met his and he smiled at her.

'I want to enjoy you,' Leo murmured huskily.

But how much longer could he withstand the onslaught on his senses? he wondered. She was driving him crazy. The complexity of this situation…the confusion of a pursuit he had never experienced and hadn't expected…made the taste of her, now that she was lying naked in his bed, all the sweeter.

His prized self-control had vanished in a puff and now, touching her… The feel of her moving under him and against him…

He'd died and gone to heaven.

He nuzzled her breasts and suckled on her brown nipples, and couldn't seem to get enough. Her skin was warm and, as he touched, she wriggled, moaning and sighing, her body slippery and supple under his hands.

The guy who had always prided himself on his artistry when it came to the pleasurable business of having sex was shaking, and in danger of losing his grip and coming before he could sink into her, which was where he wanted to be—deep inside her, filling her up.

Every little whimper of pleasure leaving her

lips took him closer and closer to the edge. He cupped the dampness between her thighs with his big hand and inserted his fingers into her, stroking slowly, and loving her wetness.

'I'm not sure how much longer I can hold on, my darling…'

'I need you too,' Kaya whispered.

And she did. Oh, how she wanted his man to fill to her and take her, soaring away to places she'd never imagined.

She'd never done this before.

The technicalities presented themselves, a wash of reality penetrating the hot haze of lust.

He was impressively built.

Kaya took deep breaths and forced herself to relax back into his caress. She sensed the urgency in him, felt its palpable weight nudging between her legs, and closed her eyes.

She knew that he was reaching for the wallet he had earlier dumped on the bedside table, and heard the tearing of the foil and then his brief withdrawal as he eased on protection.

A man who took no chances.

He entered her, long, hard and deep, and she cried out and flinched back. It was an automatic reaction. It lasted seconds but during that time she heard his exclamation of shock and then his instant withdrawal and soft cursing under his breath. When she peeked through half-closed

eyes, it was to see that he was ditching the condom that had slid off during that moment when
he had found out…what she'd been so desperate
to keep under wraps.

'Kaya!'

'What?' Kaya wriggled up a little but she just
couldn't meet his darkly demanding gaze.

'You know what. Why didn't you tell me?
You should have told me.'

The last thing he'd expected had been this.
A virgin!

And there was more. A tumult of chaotic
thoughts rumbled around in his head as he realised that in his shock, God only knew, but the
condom had not done what it should have done.
Had it torn? He'd felt his own liquid all over
his hands as he'd pulled out of her. He couldn't
dwell on that. He wouldn't. His eyes were hot
and dark as jet as he watched her looking at
him. He really *did* forget everything because,
damn it, *a virgin*. It was a shot of adrenaline. He
breathed in deeply, head thrown back, overcome
by something that felt like…*possessiveness*.

He should be worried sick about the consequences of the unforeseen. He wasn't. He was
on a high.

'Sorry,' Kaya apologised in an agonised whisper. 'I should have. You're right. I didn't want to
because… Okay, I'll go. I understand.'

'No chance,' Leo ground out, already rising to the occasion.

'What do you mean?'

'It's a turn-on, okay? Stay, Kaya. I... I'll be gentle. I can do things to you that don't involve penetration and you can do the same for me.' He shot her a crooked smile. He felt her relax, and the rush of triumph, satisfaction and pleasure that filled him made him light-headed for a couple of seconds. 'Sex can wait for...later.'

'Okay...'

Kaya smiled back and pulled him towards her.

Kaya looked at Leo. He was standing by the window, his back to her, staring out at a day that was only just waking up. They hadn't drawn the curtains and she could glimpse the rosy hue of winter in the skies, a mix of greys and blues and tinges of pink and orange.

He was naked. Naked and perfect: broad shoulders, a narrow waist and long, muscular legs liberally sprinkled with dark hair, just like his chest. All man.

He turned round and smiled slowly as their eyes met. He walked towards her and Kaya adjusted her position on the bed, eyes irresistibly drawn to the hang of his penis and its urgent swelling as he drew closer to her until, as he stood by the side of the bed, it was throbbing and hard.

In the space of four days—lazy days passed in a blur of bed, sex and some food grabbed in between—she had lost all the inhibitions that had kicked in that very first time.

He had taught her and he had taught her well. He had opened her up to a world where only touching existed and she had learned to enjoy it.

'Lick me,' he commanded huskily, and Kaya knelt on the bed, steadying herself, and took him in her mouth.

Leo looked down at her, at her head moving, her hair streaming around her.

He couldn't stop wanting her. Every time they'd made love it had been with the same driving, blind passion with which they'd made love that very first time…fully, tenderly and completely, after the mishap with the condom.

He entered her gently, nudging until she was ready to open for him. On the brink of coming as she weaved her magic with her hand and her mouth, he pulled back and joined her on the bed, first holding her close so that he could feel her heart beating against his chest and then, with some reluctance, angling her so that he could pleasure her lazily…no rush whatsoever…because work had been on hold for days, so why not a few more hours? He went between her legs and settled there, tasting her with his tongue, flicking and rousing against the stiffened nub of her clitoris and loving her increasing demands for fulfilment.

Their bodies had learnt to move in tune with one another, and when eventually he entered her she was as ready for him as he was for her.

They came, and Leo felt the soaring inside him as he arched back, something raw, powerful and...*dangerously unsettling*.

She nestled against him, sated.

'We should think about getting some work done.' He half-yawned, because it wasn't yet six-thirty and he was discovering that early-morning sex could do that to a guy, even one who was used to getting up at five, raring to go.

'Guess so. I've barely glanced at my emails for the past few days.'

'Really meant with the house.'

Manhattan, Kaya thought, *is beckoning*. Reality might have taken a break, but all breaks had to come to an end. And what happened next... for them? For her?

Had she imagined that they would live in this exciting bubble for ever? Or maybe just until he got around to thinking that he might want more than a few days of stolen pleasure?

Because the rules of the game had changed for her. She'd known him for the guy he was. He didn't want involvement, not even in the heat of the moment when people were wont to say stuff from the heart and not the head. He wasn't on the market for a relationship but *she* was.

She had feelings for this man and not just uncomplicated, superficial feelings—she had deep feelings, feelings of love, affection and tenderness. All those crazy, crazy feelings she'd been so sure she could avoid because she'd told herself that he really wasn't her type.

She had sleepwalked into a situation and it was a catastrophe. He'd woken up now—time to get going—but her? She was lost in a different place. She'd foolishly nodded off and woken up in a different world.

Heart beating fast, she edged back.

She laughed thinly. 'You're right. Can't put off the inevitable for ever!' She turned to stare at the ceiling but all she could see was his beautiful, dear face that she knew so well now. 'Julie Anne's room will take time. I'll start…today.'

Leo felt the shift of her weight away from him. He wanted to draw her back against him, and the very fact that he couldn't be bothered to get out of bed and address work concerns was worrying.

Likewise, he made some space between them. 'Excellent idea,' he murmured. 'Can't postpone what needs to be done, however seductive it is to pretend that we can.'

Two hours later, Kaya was outside the room Leo had adopted as his makeshift office. The door was shut. After so many days of feeling as one with him, waking in his arms and opening herself to him in all sorts of ways, she was now hesitant and weak with nerves.

She had to force herself to knock, push the door open and then stand in front of him as if she were suddenly at an interview waiting to be invited to have a seat.

She looked scrappy in her oldest jogging bottoms, a faded sweatshirt, hair scraped back because it had been getting in her eyes, and she was pale. She could feel it. She'd gone to Julie Anne's room to lose herself in nostalgia and sort stuff out, but she hadn't been able to run away from the chain of thought that had begun in the bedroom when he'd told her that it was time for them to start picking up the pieces of daily reality.

She wasn't going to break down, because she only had herself to blame for falling for the guy, but she'd barely been able to focus on sifting out the million and one things in the room, from paperwork and souvenirs, to clothes, shoes, favourite books and magazines with some article or other she'd thought might come in useful.

And then, at the back of the wardrobe, wedged so far in the corner than it hadn't been visible, she'd found a box. Treasured possessions: a lock of hair, some faded photos, letters...and a journal. Not for her eyes. She had clocked that within a page of reading it.

'I have something for you.' She held out the box and saw him glance at it and stiffen.

'What the hell is that?' Leo snapped.

'I found it in your mother's wardrobe, stuffed at the back. I think you should look at it. There's a journal. You need to read it.'

'What the heck for?'

Their eyes clashed.

He'd been thinking of Kaya solidly. He hadn't managed to get a scrap of work done, not an email sent, and now here she was, handing him something, and he could feel a knot of tension tighten inside him.

'I'll leave it, shall I?'

'Or you could dump it somewhere, shut the door behind you and come and let me make love to you,' Leo drawled, relaxing back in the chair, legs stretched out, hands clasped behind his head.

Arrogant, Kaya thought with helpless fascination, cocky and...*scared.*

'Read it, Leo,' she said gruffly. 'I'll be in the kitchen if you…want to talk.'

Kaya waited over an hour. She made coffee, wondered what was happening with Leo, tipped out the coffee undrunk, made some more and did the same.

She'd opened that box, expecting the usual—some trinkets, maybe some photos or else just the usual assortment of sentimental bits and pieces which Julie Anne had been fond of keeping.

The last thing she'd expected was that journal and, the second she had flipped it open and begun reading, she'd known that it was a story Leo would have to read, whatever the contents.

For it had been written by a seventeen-year-old Julie Anne, living with her parents and pregnant.

I can't believe what Mama and Papa want me to do. This is the worst day of my life. I hate them, I hate them, I hate them. Diego and I are going to run away. We can't think of anything else to do.

That had been the opening entry. Kaya had snapped shut the journal and rocked back on her heels, deep in thought, heart beating fast, knowing that what she held in her hands would be a story neither she, and more importantly Leo, had ever thought they would get.

Would either of them want to hear this story? Would it be better left untold? Sometimes the truth was far less kind than all the wild tricks the imagination could play.

Lost in thought, she was barely aware of his approach until she glanced up to see him framed in the doorway.

Under the rich bronze of his skin, he was ashen.

'You don't have to talk about it,' she said quickly.

'You should read it.'

'It's…it's none of my business.'

'It's both our business, even if the reasons behind that aren't the same. Jesus, it's still morning, but if I could, I'd hit the whisky.'

He looked at her levelly, his dark eyes deep and unfathomable, and she wished she knew what he was thinking. The chasm that had begun to yawn between them grew bigger.

'That journal…those keepsakes…' He shook his head and prowled through the kitchen, coming to rest in front of her but almost immediately moving to sit. 'A shock.'

'Life's full of them, I've discovered.'

'Yes, you had your share when you found out about me.'

Kaya wanted to ask what happened next but she knew, just as she knew that she wasn't going to hang around and wait for him to deliver the final blow to what they'd enjoyed.

'You need to…think about whatever it is you've learned, and you won't be able to do that while you're here.'

The silence stretched to breaking point, then he said quietly, 'Agreed. I don't… I don't need reminders of a past that's suddenly taken shape and come to life. I see the bigger picture now. I see the canvas that was painted over thirty years ago and…yes… I need to digest that. Away from here.'

'Then go. It's what you need to do.'

'I still want you.'

'That's not how this goes.'

'There's no recipe for how relationships go or how they end. I have a place in the Bahamas. I would have space to think. Read the journal, Kaya, and come with me. We have a connection that can't be replicated with anyone else. And, even though my head's telling me it's time to go, my body is telling me we need to continue this or else we'll both regret cutting it short too soon.'

'I don't think so, Leo.' Kaya barely recognised the tough, hard edge in her voice but she could feel the barriers falling into place. 'It's been fun, and now we need to call it a day.'

'Is that what you really want? You really want us to walk away from one another before this thing has run its course?'

'I prefer to leave things on a high.' She forced a smile. 'Instead of it fizzling away into disappointment and boredom.'

Leo lowered his eyes, shielding his expression, and Kaya could sense his withdrawal. She was already missing him, missing the easy familiarity that had crept up on them from nowhere. How desperately she wanted that back, but for what? A week or two more of falling even deeper and harder for him? She'd learnt too many lessons in disappointment from her mother to go down that road.

'Your choice,' was what he drawled when he raised his eyes to look at her. 'And no need to rush with packing. I can wrap things up here remotely, I imagine.' His expression gentled. 'And, Kaya, the halfway house? You were worried—don't be. It won't be sold. I will hold it in a safe trust and, rest assured, whatever investment is needed to keep it afloat, to expand it, will be undertaken. Whatever has happened in the past, and whatever my feelings about my mother, her legacy there will be protected.'

And that's why I love you. Because you're a

decent guy. You're not a rich bastard, you're a decent guy who can never love... And I can't be the one who loves for both of us.

'Thank you.'

CHAPTER SEVEN

LEO HAD BEEN staring out of the window of his magnificent villa in the sunshine for forty minutes…he checked his Rolex: no forty-eight minutes…when his mobile phone pinged.

What the hell was he doing?

He had hit Manhattan two weeks ago, energised with positive thoughts. No Kaya but, then again, for the best—no tears and no pleading were an added bonus. The best break-up a guy could ask for!

And work? So much of it was waiting for him that it made his eyes water when he thought about it. He would lose himself in his work. There were deals to be done, money to be made. It never failed when it came to nailing one hundred percent of his attention.

The business with the journal, the back story to his adoption…how could he not take some comfort from knowing the details? A frightened teenager pregnant and facing the wrath of her wealthy, conservative, well-connected parents... The decision to run away with his father, the Mexican immigrant who had been working on her father's sprawling estate in the Hamptons...

He had opened that journal and been consumed by the journey his mother had made. He had read and re-read about the headlong rush to freedom and the accident that had taken his father, leaving Julie Anne alone with a baby on the way and no choice but to return to the very place she had been trying to escape.

Depressed for years, isolated and at the mercy of decisions made on her behalf, she had handed Leo over, her parents had assured her, to a loving couple who would look after him the way he deserved to be looked after. She had believed them.

He hadn't been abandoned, as he had thought. Questions had been answered.

Fired up to put the business of his fling with Kaya behind him, because life was full of blips—even invigorating ones—he had quickly realised that the blip had taken more of a toll than he'd expected.

He had no idea why returning to his comfort zone had failed to settle his feverish thoughts. So they'd parted company—it wasn't the end of the world! Had she taken up lodgings in his head because he still wanted her, because for the first time in his life he was having to deal with a woman breaking it off when he'd been happy to carry on?

Surely he couldn't be that egotistic?

But he hadn't been able to focus. He'd scrolled through his phone, idly looking at numbers of women who would bite his hand off for a call from him, and had found himself deleting their contact details.

He missed her.

Sitting in his towering offices in the city, staring down at life happening eighteen storeys below, he was sucker-punched by the realisation that *he missed her.* Not just the sex but *her*— all the things that made her, the sum total of all the parts. He missed her smile, her laughter and her annoying habit of arguing with him and just never giving up.

He missed her optimism and the way she had of being supportive without saying anything at all. And he missed the person he'd been with her, as though a weight had been lifted from his shoulders. Laughter had come more easily and so had relaxation.

If she'd felt the same, she would have called.

She hadn't, although he had checked his phone on the hour to see if he'd missed any-thing. He hadn't. She would have called and the fact that she hadn't made it all the more imperative that he not be the one to crack.

Pride was an ingrained hurdle too vast to overcome and Leo saw no reason why he should try. He never had before. Nothing had changed, not really. Things started and then they ended. That was the way of the world. If there were feelings there, swirling under the surface, then he would get past them.

However, despite every assertive lecture he gave himself, he couldn't really seem to get past the reality of her abrupt absence, and after two weeks here he was, in a villa he rarely visited. From the air-conditioned splendour of the space he had tailor-made for work purposes when he'd first bought the place, he could stare out at glorious blue skies, even more glorious turquoise ocean and the expanse of icing-sugar sand that separated sea from the sloping incline to his property. Directly in front of him was his infinity pool, basking just beyond swaying palm trees.

It was a magnificent view, which Leo barely took in as he stared out, for a few seconds barely registering the beep of his mobile and only picking it up after a couple of minutes. He was pretty certain it was going to be work-related, even though only a select handful of people had this particular number.

Her name... It didn't instantly register. He wondered whether he had seen it at all but, yes, he blinked and there it was: *Kaya*.

And, just like that, the tenor of the morning suddenly changed. He opened the message and read it. She wondered where he was...was he in Manhattan...? She would like to meet, if possible.

Leo smiled a slow, curving smile of utter satisfaction. So, it hadn't just been him. He hadn't been alone in concluding that what they'd had was too good to throw away just yet. He hadn't stopped wanting her and she hadn't stopped wanting him. Why else would she have texted? Why else would she now be desperate to meet up?

He waited a while to reply, giving it an hour, when he strolled outside and admired the scenery he hadn't previously really noticed.

His reply was as brief a communication as hers had been: he was in the Bahamas, as it happened. Sure, if she wanted to meet up, why not? He would ensure arrangements were made and his PA would be in touch with the details...

Two days, was his instruction to his PA in Manhattan—that was how long he was prepared to wait to see Kaya. Long enough to show her that time hadn't stopped still for him...that he was a busy guy as he always had been; that, sure, he could fit her in but clearly not at the drop of a hat…yet not so long that he ran the risk of her changing her mind. That was the last thing he wanted.

Still smiling, Leo realised that it was possible to focus under tropical skies after all…

Buzzing up high in the sky as the helicopter whirred its way to Harbour Island a mere fifty-four hours after she had sent her text to Leo, Kaya closed her eyes and contemplated the prospect ahead of her.

Her head was spinning and her heart, which she had been so determined to put into cold storage, was fluttering madly inside her.

This situation had seemed a lot more manageable from the safety of back home, with a vast ocean between her and Leo. It had been easy to be sensible from a distance. Of course, she hadn't known where she would find him when she'd texted him on the number he had given her when life had been all sunshine and laughter between them, and she had been surprised when he had replied that he was at his villa in the Bahamas.

Yes, he'd told her that, but deep down she hadn't quite believed it. Leo chilling out in the sunshine? She hadn't seen it but she'd been wrong.

She hadn't asked why. Hadn't asked how come he wasn't in New York, to where he had bustled off within an hour of reading that journal and deciding that it was time to clear off. Wasn't he the committed workaholic, after all?

There had been no superfluous chit-chat by text, and he hadn't asked why she'd suddenly decided to pay him a visit when, two weeks before, she had turned her back on him.

Of course, Kaya knew the reason for his lack of interrogation. He figured she had read the journal, been moved, had re-examined her decision not to sleep with him again…essential, because things had to fizzle out of their own accord…and had decided to make contact.

He had cockily assumed that she just couldn't resist his charm and had had to get in touch, pathetically hoping he'd reconsider and carry her back, caveman-style, to his bed.

Leo was in for a shock.

Kaya tried to train herself to think without emotion, because a lack of emotion was what she was going to need, but it was so hard. It was especially hard now that the journey to see him was nearing its end. She didn't feel prepared. At least, not *enough*.

With a hitched sigh, she looked down at a swirling panorama of blue and white: sky and puffy clouds, the sort of to where place people went to relax and have fun.

Not for her.

She didn't quite know when, amongst all of this chaos and unhappiness, she'd suddenly realised that her period was late. And then she quickly realised a few other things as well: the metallic taste in her mouth; the way she'd gone off coffee; those little bouts of nausea...

She had known what the result of that pregnancy test would be before she'd taken it and yet, when it was confirmed, she had still frantically done three more and, with each successive positive, she'd felt a little sicker as her world dismantled in front of her.

And her choices? Few.

Certainly, there was no question that Leo would have to be told—he deserved it.

She had taken a couple of days to come to terms with the *everything*, then she had texted him.

She'd decided clearly on how to handle things. She would be calm, matter-of-fact, reasonable and undemanding.

The one thing she would not do was become emotional, because this situation demanded a cool head.

Yet here she was. The whole cool-headed approach had disappeared roughly when the plane had started climbing for take-off. She surfaced now with the realisation that the helicopter was dipping, swinging in an arc, its rotor blades slowing. When she looked out of the tiny window, it was to find it circling over an illuminated circle, with a giant 'H' marking the spot where it had to land.

Leo's villa. Her mouth went dry.

She steeled herself as the helicopter ground to a complete stop and then there was gradual silence as the blades stopped whirring then, as the door was pushed open, superseded by the call of insects that was nothing like anything she had ever heard before.

For a few seconds, standing in the open air, readying to disembark, Kaya closed her eyes and just listened. Insects called one another, high and shrill, and mingled with the throaty undertone of frogs, all competing with the rustle of warm breeze through lush shrubbery.

And then his voice…low, velvety and darkly, sexily familiar.

Her eyes flew open, adjusted and then there he was, larger than life and a lot more drop-dead gorgeous than she remembered. He was framed in the doorway of a villa that was picture-perfect, from what she could make out in the enveloping darkness, for out here, with only the light from the stars and the moon, it was inky-black.

'So you came...'

There was mild amusement in his drawl and Kaya was galvanised into motion as he strolled towards her.

He was in a pair of loose, draw-string linen trousers, an old tee-shirt and some flip-flops and he looked more eye wateringly gorgeous than he ever had.

Her mouth went dry, her heart sped up and she hurried down the stunted metal steps just in case he decided to help her down. She wasn't sure if she could face the physical contact.

Behind her, the young, enthusiastic pilot, who had done his best to engage her interest on the brief hop to the island, followed with her bag. There was a moment's reprieve while Leo chatted to him, leaving her time to gather her thoughts and pay some attention to her surroundings.

The dark shapes of the bushes, foliage and silhouettes of the tall, gently waving coconut trees were glorious. She glanced at the villa, which wasn't outrageously big, but perfectly proportioned, pink and white with a wide, wooden veranda encircling the entire property like a bracelet. The gardens appeared to be extensive and partially landscaped, and she could smell the salty tang of the sea and hear the rise and fall of waves behind all the other unfamiliar sounds.

There was some laughter and a few more pleasantries between Leo and the pilot, and then the helicopter was weaving its way back up, up, up and away, leaving the two of them together.

The silence was broken by Leo. He didn't move towards her. He kept his distance, leading her into the villa, which was a marvel of tropical architecture. The blonde wooden flooring was interrupted by colourful rugs, and the breeze blowing through the shutters was helped along by ceiling fans.

'So…' he drawled, leading the way towards the kitchen. 'You're here.'

He faced her, his dark eyes skewering her to the spot and, in return, Kaya looked at him and tried not to drink him in, because she'd forgotten how much he meant to her, and how familiar she was with every angle and contour of his handsome face.

'Yes.' The bracing, impersonal speech she had rehearsed—which would have been followed by a swift escape to bed, having confirmed her return flight for Canada the following day—had vanished, leaving her to struggle with the business of actually being in his presence.

'There's no need to look so terrified,' Leo said wryly. 'I happen to be very glad that you changed your mind. You look good, Kaya.' He cleared his throat and briefly looked away before returning his dark gaze to her face. 'Sit. I'll get you a drink.'

'No! No, thank you.'

Leo's eyebrows shot up.

Not the reaction he was expecting. Actually, her visible discomfort was not at all what he'd been expecting. Possibly a bit too soon to fall into each other's arms, all things considered, but he had banked on more enthusiasm. Or perhaps it was his imagination playing tricks on him. After all, she *had* made the first move.

'It'll relax you,' he drawled, but he remained where he was, staring at her from under his lashes. 'I haven't dragged you here, Kaya.'

'I realise that.'

'Do you want me to coax you out of whatever sudden bout of uncertainty you're going through? Want me to tell you how glad I am you're here? Want me to beg you not to have a change of heart?'

'Would you? Beg me to stay? Because I don't remember you doing that when you left.'

Kaya could have kicked herself for having said that, so she tacked on in a harried undertone, 'But, no. I don't want you to do any of those things, as it happens. I'm here of my own volition and I won't be having a change of heart. I'll have some water, please.'

'You read the journal.'

'Yes.' Kaya could relax with this. With this, she could feel her anxiety and trepidation disappear under a wave of extreme sympathy for this wonderful, generous guy with all that baggage that had made him the wary, hands-off man he was. 'I'm sorry, Leo. It must have broken your heart to have read about your mother.'

Leo flushed darkly.

Unaccustomed to sharing anything of himself or his feelings, he opened his mouth to shut down the conversation, but he didn't. He remembered what this was all about, this spell she seemed to have over him. It was still there because he heard himself admit gruffly, 'It was… good to have some answers.'

'And yet you must wonder what might have been if she had sought you out. Or vice versa.'

'Pointless to dwell on something that didn't happen and now never will. But, like I said, it was good to know that…'

'That although you ended up in foster care, it wasn't because Julie Anne had put you there. No, she had been fed a lie by her parents. She had thought you were going to a good home. So really, you weren't dumped, were you? Not really. Not as you described it to me once?'

'Did I?' Leo shrugged.

'You did,' Kaya told him gently. She momentarily left behind the anxiety over her reasons for being here and was caught up in the moment. Her heart swelled with tenderness for him, even though she knew that that very tenderness was a weakness she had to control.

Lord only knew what Leo had felt when he had read what Julie Anne had endured, but he was right—questions had been answered and for him it surely must have been sweet release to know that were it not for tragic circumstances, he would never have been given up for adoption.

And good for him to know that, as atonement for something she'd felt she could never rectify, Julie Anne had moved to the great British Columbian wilderness, disowned her parents—only taking with her the legacy left by her maternal grandmother—and devoted her life to doing good.

True to his word, the halfway house was already in the process of being modernised.

'But we're not here to discuss my past, are we? That's not why you came, is it?'

He strolled across to the imposing American-style fridge to fetch her some water, and Kaya felt her tension levels ratchet up as reality reasserted itself.

*No, they weren't here to discuss his past—
far from it.*

His fingers brushed hers as he handed her the
glass, and heat flooded her.

'This is a beautiful place, Leo.'

'Isn't it? My first purchase after my first million. Two important firsts.'

'Lucky you, being able to afford somewhere
like this. Do you come here often?' Kaya knew
that she was buying time, which was pointless,
because there was only so long she could do
that.

'When I can. I find that relaxation has never
been my thing, having bought somewhere spe-
cifically tailored for that very purpose. I over-
estimated my need for down time.'

'I was surprised when you told me that you
were here. I guess I didn't see you actually
going through with that plan. I don't know why.'

'It was a last-minute decision.'

He flushed at the admission because it reminded him of why he was here: too much over-
thinking for a guy who preferred action; too
much getting lost in a whole lot of memories
about what had felt so good, and missing the
woman who had done that—the woman sitting
in his kitchen, warily watching him as though
he might pounce at any minute. And that journal playing on his mind—those little clips of

things his mother had secreted away in a box, hiding her past from prying eyes.

He'd left it all behind, and had seen no point in dragging the past into his present, but he had not been able to leave those feelings behind him. He had spent a lifetime bitterly side-lining the woman who had chosen to abandon him, and he had had to revisit those assumptions and make his peace with a completely new image of her.

His life had been put in a spin cycle, and not even the familiarity of the high-octane fast lane waiting for him in New York had been able to clear his head. So he'd come here. Except, he could do without being reminded of that fact, because it signalled a weakness he found hard to accept in himself. It smacked of running away.

This wasn't how he had foreseen their first few hours panning out: Kaya sitting in guarded, monosyllabic wariness at the kitchen table while his mood plummeted ever deeper into incomprehension and impatience.

He smiled slowly, wolfishly, and strolled towards her until he towered over her and she looked up at him. It was there. He could see it—the low, burning flame of desire—and he felt a kick of triumph, because this was what he felt comfortable with. He knew how to deal with this. He could handle the physical a lot better than he could handle the turmoil of emotions.

He'd had to deal with an onslaught of emotions recently, and now seemed just about the right time to put such annoyances to bed.

With a good following wind. And *soon*—the sooner the better.

He stroked the side of her face, a lazy trail on her satin-smooth cheek, and his nostrils flared as he saw her eyes wide and her eyelids flutter.

'I don't know how I could have forgotten how beautiful you are, Kaya,' he murmured huskily, moving to pull a chair close, and sitting so that he was more or less straddling her chair, his thighs on the outside of hers, his finger still on her cheek, not breaking that physical connection. He contoured her mouth with his finger, tugged the softness of her lower lip and then let that wandering finger go further, tracing a path along her neck, across her shoulders and then over the tee-shirt that was just about snug enough for him to conjure up the ripeness of her breasts, the way her nipples swelled to his touch.

'Leo...'

'I've missed the way you say my name.' He dipped his hand down, down, down...and pushed it gently underneath the tee-shirt until he was cupping her thin bra...and cursing the fact that she had worn one, because he was so turned on by her that he didn't want the impediment of any restrictive clothing between them.

Kaya heard his words go over her head. Her mind was foggy and all she was conscious of was his touch. The way he made her body feel, the way he could make it sing… Lord, how she'd missed that—missed *him* and missed *that*.

In a trance, her mind emptied and she sighed and tilted her body back in the chair, conscious of him easing down her bra so that it was underneath one breast, pushing it up.

Her eyes were closed and her lips were parted as he rolled up the tee-shirt, taking his time, then closing his mouth over her nipple and flicking his tongue across the sensitive surface as he suckled and pulled it into his mouth.

She was drowning, clutching the seat of the chair until her knuckles were white, and she slid a little lower as he continued to suckle.

In her mind, she pictured the raw beauty of his body, hard for her, throbbing in its need. She half-opened her eyes, saw his dark head moving at her breast and the fog began to clear. Horror replaced pleasure. How could all that tension, anxiety and sickening panic be swept away by one touch?

She froze for a couple of seconds and then wriggled away. When she glanced down, when he detached from her breast, she saw that her nipple was slick with the wetness of his mouth and she dragged her tee-shirt down without bothering with the bra.

'Kaya…' He groaned, flinging himself back into the chair and closing his eyes for a few seconds. When he opened them to look at her, there was naked desire in the slumberous depths of his dark eyes.

'That shouldn't have happened!'

'What are you talking about? I need you. You need me. Let's go to bed. Let's make love.'

'This isn't… Leo…' Kaya swept shaky fingers through her hair. She was appalled by her weakness, appalled by how quickly he had been able to rouse her, appalled by how shamefully eagerly she had succumbed to his caresses.

'What's the matter? You don't know what you're doing to me.'

'You think I've come here to pick up where we left off?'

'Haven't you? Because that's what your body was telling me a minute ago.'

Kaya stared at him in speechless silence. So much for all the mental preparation she'd tried to do. None of it had been worth a penny the second he had decided to touch her.

She edged back as far as she could, terrified that he would reach out again, ninety percent sure she would have the strength to resist, but terrified that there was still that ten percent that would abandon everything just to have him touch her.

But wasn't that what love did—made her weak and helpless? She'd never really believed that until now, until she was in the grip of its power.

'I haven't come for sex, Leo.'

'Why else would you be here, Kaya?' Leo frowned, utterly perplexed and physically aching from his libido having to climb down from its excruciating high.

Kaya breathed in deeply and felt faint. She weakened, luxuriating in the fantasy that he loved her, that this was a normal situation... that they were lovers waking up to the beauty of becoming parents together.

The fantasy didn't last.

'Leo, I know I didn't have to come here to tell you this face to face, but I didn't think it was something I could convey over the phone, or worse, by text...'

Kaya watched the way he went very still and, before he could start guessing games, allowing her unconsciously to dodge the obvious, she said, quietly, 'Leo, I'm pregnant.'

She saw every flicker of emotion he tried to conceal, from puzzlement that he might have misheard what she had said, all the way through to dawning comprehension, shock and then, inevitably, disbelief.

'You're kidding.'

'I've never been more serious. Why would I come all the way over here to spin you a fairy story?'

'But it's not possible!'

'It happened. I'm pregnant, Leo, and, much as I knew that this wasn't going to be what you wanted to hear, I couldn't keep something this big from you.'

'No, you *can't be*.'

Who was he kidding? Leo looked at the gravity of her expression and knew in a heartbeat that she was telling the truth.

She was as straight as an arrow and honest to a fault.

She was pregnant. He was going to be a father and life as he knew it was going to come to an end.

He could continue thinking of various different ways of transmitting his incredulity and shock but what would be the point of that? Reality was going to remain the same, however much he tried to push it aside.

The room suddenly felt too small…the villa felt too small…the world he'd known was closing in on him and he vaulted to his feet, his movements jerky and lacking in their usual grace.

'When did you find out?' He turned to look at her.

'A few days ago.'

'What a mess.' He rubbed his eyes with the pads of his thumbs.

'I'm sorry.' In none of her wildest dreams had Kaya ever contemplated something that could be a joyous event turning out like this. She had always had such regimented plans for her life, plans that would avoid her ending up in a place where she was vulnerable, and yet what had she gone and done? Fallen hard for someone who didn't want her for anything but sex; someone who was incapable of sharing his heart and soul with another person. Someone who could leave that journal behind.

'Why? It takes two to tango, as they say.' Leo vaulted upright and raked his fingers through his hair. 'I think I need something very stiff.'

'Yes,' Kaya murmured, arresting him before he could head off to get the drink he felt he needed. 'A stiff drink is just what you need for the mess you're now in.' She placed her hand protectively on her stomach and banked down the searing hurt inside her.

'My apologies,' Leo muttered. 'This has come as a shock.'

'And a very unpleasant one, from the looks of it,' Kaya said with raw emotion, tilting her chin at a defiant angle. 'You think your life is over. You think… Maybe you think that you won't be the free bachelor you were before. You're wrong. I came here to tell you about the pregnancy because you deserved to know. I didn't come here to try and pin you down or force you to change your lifestyle! I would never do that. I would never be so selfish, especially when I've known from the beginning that you're not a guy who wants longevity when it comes to relationships.'

She bunched her hands into clenched fists.

'Come again?'

Kaya reddened. He looked utterly shocked at her outburst, but why should she hold back? It was obvious that he didn't want this baby and was appalled at the grenade that had detonated in his carefully ordered life.

And that hurt. It really did.

'You heard me, Leo,' she persisted stubbornly. 'I'm not asking you to give up anything for me. This isn't about sacrifice for you, this is about you deserving to have a role in your baby's life if that's what you would want.'

He returned to sit opposite her and his dark eyes were as cold as the wintry depths of Sibe-

ria. 'If that's your message, you have some serious re-thinking to do on that.'

'What do you mean?'

'Do you honestly imagine that I'm going to
deal with this situation by…what? Throwing
money at it and walking away, because I don't
want my bachelor lifestyle interrupted?'

'I never said that…'

'It's the implication.'

'Of course I don't expect you to walk away.
I know, after everything you've been through,
Leo, that that's not a route you would want to
take. But I'm just giving you the option, just
letting you know that I'm not trying to corner
you into doing anything you don't want to do…'
She breathed in deeply but, when she released
her breath, it was on a shudder. 'I would never
stop you from visiting your child. If I were that
kind of person, then I wouldn't be here in the
first place.'

'That's very generous of you, Kaya, but I have
a completely different scenario in mind.'

'What's that?'

'Marriage.'

CHAPTER EIGHT

Kaya was momentarily lost for words. Her mouth fell open and she stared at him in shocked, confused consternation.

'Marriage?'

'Correct.'

'Us? Me and you?'

'I'm not seeing anyone else here, are you?' Leo made a show of looking round the room in search of someone lurking behind furniture.

'That's crazy,' Kaya said.

'Why?'

'Because we aren't in a relationship, Leo.'

'What are you talking about?'

'We broke up,' she told him flatly. 'We had a fling and we broke up—or maybe you don't remember that bit. This was never about love and marriage and making a go of things. This was all about the sex and nothing else.' Just verbalising their situation was like swallowing glass. Every word hurt because every word reminded her just how different it was for her. She hated herself for half-hoping that he would contradict what she'd said. She hated herself for clinging to illusions.

'What does that have to do with the fact that you're pregnant? Yes, I know what we had was a fling, Kaya, and I realise it wasn't meant to stay the course—but things change and a pregnancy changes everything.'

'A pregnancy doesn't change the fact that we don't…don't…love one another, Leo.'

'This is no longer about the two of us and what we want or don't want.'

Kaya could feel his eyes on her and she couldn't meet his unflinching gaze because he saw far too much for her liking. And there was no way she wanted him to see into her head, to see the unhappiness wrapped around her, because she loved this man and he didn't love her back.

She didn't want anyone to feel sorry for her, and he would feel sorry for her. He would try and hide his dismay, but of course he would remind her of what she already knew: she had disobeyed the ground rules. He would gently tell her that he didn't return those feelings and never would. It was probable that the horror of attaching himself to a woman who wanted what he couldn't give would have him running for the hills and doing just as she'd anticipated—money without commitment. Shared responsibility but, beyond that, nothing at all. And, every single time she saw him, she would see the pity in his eyes and she would be hurt all over again.

No thanks.

She had her pride, and her heart was beating like a sledgehammer inside her as she tried not to be swept along by logic that worked for him but not for her.

'But it really is, Leo,' she said coolly. 'And it should be. A marriage should never start on the basis of a sacrifice being made, and a child would never benefit, caught between parents shackled together for the wrong reasons.'

'Shackled?'

'Isn't that what we would be if we were to marry without love and without shared dreams? When people start off life together with a child at the centre of it, shouldn't there be hope and love? Shouldn't it be an adventure for both of them and, even if the adventure doesn't work out in the end—and often it doesn't—isn't it important that it's at least there at the start?'

'I'm afraid I don't share your romantic dreams,' Leo said coolly.

'They're not romantic dreams.'

Leo clicked his tongue, impatient to hustle the conversation along to where he wanted it to go.

Neither of them had predicted this but a way through the morass would have to be found. He wasn't going to gracefully retire from responsibility because it suited her. She might be in search of the perfect fairy tale but there was no way their child was going to pay the price for her pursuing that particular dream.

But he couldn't force her hand, and neither did he want to. He could think of nothing worse than dragging a reluctant bride to the altar so that she could become a reluctant and resentful parent, waiting for their marriage to implode.

What a mess.

He raked his fingers through his hair and pressed his thumbs against his eyes. When he looked at her once more, there was genuine empathy in her eyes.

'We're on opposite sides of a great divide,' he conceded heavily. 'I know what it's like to grow up without parents, a number in a system. I never thought about having children but, now that I am to be a father, one thing I know is that I intend to give my child everything it is within my power to give.'

'Are you saying that, unless I do as you say, you'd fight me for custody?' Kaya asked sharply.

'You're doing it again.'

'Doing what?'

'Over-dramatising. Kaya. I would never do

that but, by hook or by crook, we're going to have to navigate a way through this—one that meets both our needs.' He paused. 'You want to have the perfect life. You want romance and sweet dreams, and a bucket list of other stuff that usually falls by the wayside before the ink on the marriage certificate's had time to dry.'

'That's so cynical!'

'It's realistic.' He waved his hand dismissively, but when he looked at her something inside him twisted, because he was going to have to be the guy who put a torch to those dreams. He remembered the way she'd looked after they'd made love: face open and flushed, her eyes drowsy and tender. He remembered her laughter, the ring of it that always made him smile.

This wasn't about memory lane, he told himself. It wasn't about getting trapped in mushy nonsense. This was about a baby coming and some hard decisions having to be made.

By hook or by crook, using whatever means at his disposal he saw fit.

'You want to go your own way and pursue your game plan to find the perfect guy, but for me the thought of another man having a say in the upbringing of my own flesh and blood is anathema. What about you?'

'What about me...? What does that mean?'

Kaya was diverted by thinking who this other man was likely to be when the only man she wanted was sitting right opposite her.

Would there ever *be* another man—one who didn't end up always being *second best*?

Yet to agree to Leo's proposal risked so much potential for hurt. When she thought about seeing him every day—being near him, living with him and, who knew?, sleeping with him until such time as it all fizzled out—her heart wanted to break into a million pieces because it would be a life of constant pain. The pain of unrequited love.

He was right—it was an almighty mess—and yet, when she thought of the tiny life inside her, she was filled with love, protectiveness and absolute joy.

Caught up in a tangle of thoughts, Kaya surfaced to hear him saying something about marriage.

'I just can't think about marrying you, Leo.'

'So you've already said. I was asking what you thought about the fact that *I*, like you, would eventually marry. It was never on the agenda, like I said, but if I had a child… I would want them to have what I never had and it's called a nuclear family.'

Leo was being honest. He was a guy who had always envisaged himself walking alone through life but, now that fate had thrown a spanner in the works, then marriage and a partner was inevitable. His starting point would just be different from hers: he would be going into it with his eyes wide open.

'You...marry...?'

'Of course. And I imagine it would be sooner rather than later.' His voice was casual but his narrowed eyes were sharp. He picked up the shock in her voice as she was forced to envisage something slightly different from whatever scenario had been playing out in her head. Well...wasn't all fair in love and war? It wasn't as though he was fabricating anything, although it wouldn't hurt to bring the timeline for this sudden marriage-to-a-suitable-woman idea forward by a few years...

'You can't just pluck a candidate from a line-up and put a ring on her finger, Leo.'

'That's not how it would work for *you*, because you would insist on your "ideal, for-ever guy" checklist. For me, take love out of the equation and I'll be perfectly happy to have a partner I get along well enough with, who doesn't expect what can't be given but appreciates what can, and is happy to be a mother to my child. I wouldn't be fussy with the detail and I wouldn't be looking for the impossible.' He smiled to cement his point.

Kaya felt the colour drain from her face. It was a realistic scenario. This was a man who wasn't on the hunt for love and wouldn't see marriage to an amenable and appreciative woman as making do. He would see it as perfectly acceptable.

And when he said sooner rather than later...? She could imagine the queue of woman who would give their eye teeth to have Leo's ring on their finger. She could imagine more than that. She could imagine how it would feel to share custody with him and his newly acquired wife. To know that, as much as he'd said he would hate the thought of another man being involved in the upbringing of his flesh and blood, she too would hate another woman having a say in her child.

'Of course,' Leo resumed briskly, leaving her to stew in the perfectly plausible scenario he had created, 'I would insist on a very generous maintenance package.'

'Of course,' Kaya said faintly.

Which led her down another alley, one that led to their child having to balance extreme privilege—which he or she would encounter on every trip to visit Leo—and a far more modest situation with her because she could never feather her nest at Leo's expense.

And how would their child feel, should he

or she ever find out that she had rejected marriage in favour of singledom? Deprived? Angry? Judgemental? All of the above?

'We can carry on this conversation in the morning,' Leo said helpfully and Kaya blinked.

'I'd actually planned on returning home tomorrow,' she confessed.

'I'm afraid that won't be happening.'

'But I've said everything I came to say.' Had she? Yes, of course she had, although with what he had just said he'd thrown a curve ball, and she was reeling from it.

'In which case, I'll do all the talking.'

He rose to his feet and stood back, a towering and imposing figure, eyes flinty-hard, allowing no argument.

'I hadn't quite foreseen your surprise visit turning out like this,' Leo admitted, flushing and shoving his hands into the pockets of his loose linen trousers. 'But all the bedrooms are prepared. You can choose which you'd like.'

Kaya stood up as well, hot, bothered and in a muddle she should have foreseen but hadn't. She knew what he'd expected, and the thought of them together in bed made her body burn and filled her with a yearning she didn't want or need.

'It's late.' His voice gentled. 'Yes, it's been a shock to me, but I hope I haven't worn you out by insisting on thrashing this…situation…out without you first catching up on your sleep.' He looked at her hesitantly. 'I… You should have something to eat. I expect, er, you must be hungrier than usual…or are you?'

'Hungrier than usual?'

'In your…condition.'

'I'm okay. I… I'll take some water up, please.'

'Tomorrow I'll show you around the island,' he murmured.

'I haven't come to take in the sights.' Kaya dredged up some asperity to remind herself that this was no longer about emotion but about business.

Leo paused to look at her. 'What else do you suggest, Kaya? That we sit in here, working out the complexities of this situation like two business associates thrashing out a thorny deal? We were lovers. We were also, I'd like to think, friends. We can surely communicate whilst having a tour of the island and making an attempt to relax in one another's company?' He remembered how she'd yielded in his arms earlier, her body betraying her, telling him how much she still fancied him.

Kaya nodded.

'Don't worry,' he said without inflection in his voice. 'There's a way forward to be found and, whether we approach the situation as business acquaintances or ex-lovers, that way will be found. I've said what I had to say on the matter of my idea of a solution, which you've refused, so...' he shrugged '...we'll work a way past that to something satisfactory. And then I'll have you delivered back to Nassau for a flight to Vancouver.

'I'll bring your bag up and show you to the bedrooms. Like I said, take your pick.'

Kaya woke the following morning, alert to her surroundings and without the luxury of any temporary amnesia as to where she was and why she was there.

She'd barely taken in her surroundings the evening before but now she did. She slipped off the bed and stared. The bedroom suite was huge. The bed was the size of a football field. The wardrobes were all built-in, indigo-blue and, as with everywhere else in the villa, the floor was a marvel of pale wood.

She strolled to the bank of windows, pulled open the wooden shutters and gazed out at a sprawling panorama of greens in every shade. Manicured lawns undulated to a distant strip of swaying coconut trees and, beyond the trees, she could glimpse a ribbon of blue sea. There was a refreshing coolness to the breeze and a fragrance to it that made her nostrils flare. It was the fragrance of a thousand different kinds of shrub, bush and flower and, across the lawns, she could make out those very flowers and see splashes of vivid colour, oranges, reds and yellows spilling out of giant pots and clambering around the trees.

The veranda, which tempted her to go outside via a door built into an archway next to the windows, was broad and sheltered and there were chairs and low sofas dotted here and there.

It was the stuff that dreams were made of—not appropriate, given the nightmare she had brought to his door.

She thought back to his reaction. He'd been shocked but he had risen to the occasion without blinking an eye. He had proposed marriage—for him a telling sacrifice, something that showed how serious he was about taking responsibility. She had thrown his offer back at him, but he hadn't tried to force her hand, even though she knew that driving him would be his own past experiences of making it on his own without the support of family—a number in an institution going it alone. It had trained him to go it alone for the rest of his life until she'd rocked his world with an unplanned pregnancy.

Her bag looked sad, small and vulnerable sitting on the ground by the wardrobes. She got dressed quickly. She didn't know what the day held in store. She'd brought precious few clothes with her—a stern reminder that she wasn't off on some kind of exotic tropical holiday—but she was concerned at how sparse her supply was, some underwear and some random light clothes, last worn last summer and various summers before that.

She looked around her as she headed for the kitchen. The villa really was very big. All the rooms were super-sized and the flow of cool, blonde wood, shutters and faded Persian rugs emphasised the space. The art on the walls was all local, colourful and vibrant. For a house that was apparently seldom used, it was comfortable and luxurious at the same time.

She heard Leo before she saw him, hearing the sound of him in the kitchen, the pad of footsteps and the clattering of crockery.

Heart suddenly pounding, Kaya slowed her pace and then, once at the kitchen door, simply stood and looked at him for a few stolen seconds when his back was turned as he busied himself at a high-tech coffee machine on the counter.

He was so beautiful—tall, athletic yet as graceful as a jungle animal. He was in a pair of low-slung khaki shorts and an old tee-shirt. He was barefoot and he looked fabulously, carelessly elegant.

She cleared her throat.

Leo turned. Of course he'd sensed her approach, *sensed* that she was in the kitchen, before she chose to make her presence known. When she had first texted him, told him that she wanted to see him, he had assumed it would be a straightforward case of picking up where they had left off, and he'd been elated at the thought of that. Having spent two weeks asking himself questions he couldn't answer, and feeling things that made no sense, it had been a relief to be presented with what he understood: sex. An affair. Passion.

But then to be told that he was going to be a father... He'd felt shock, the bottom falling out of his world, a future he had never factored into his present and something else: the stirring of masculine pride, a sense of joy and the need for this woman carrying his child to be the one at his side.

He had offered marriage, and he was ashamed to admit that it hadn't occurred to him that she wouldn't accept his offer. Why not? She'd acted as though it was a tawdry business transaction, but it wasn't. They'd been lovers and he still turned her on, and what more glue was there for a relationship than a baby?

But then, how could he have forgotten that she didn't jump to the same tune as all those other women he had dated in the past? She was her own person; she had turned him down flat and there was nothing he could do about it.

She wanted what he was incapable of giving: love. He'd never been taught how to do that, how to love. He'd been taught how to survive, how to conquer and how to be self-reliant.

Yes, that journal had put a completely different spin on things, had made him revise the circumstances of his past, but too much had been etched in stone to be reversed. Abandonment had turned him into a self-contained fortress and that was something he couldn't reverse.

Love wasn't in his remit.

Which didn't mean that he was going to give up on his determination to keep them together as a family. To marry her.

He would just have to adopt a different approach.

If he couldn't explain the advantages of staying together, then he would have to show her. He would have to lead her to the very conclusion he wanted. He would have to entice her to come to him, because he couldn't and would never force her to do anything against her will.

He looked at her, expression shuttered, for a few silent seconds. She was long, brown, slender and stunning in a washed out yellow dress with thin straps that fell shapelessly to her knees. And she was wearing trainers with thin socks.

With not much effort, he could have kept staring at her until he embarrassed himself.

'How did you sleep?'

Leo broke eye contact and returned to the coffee, but he was aware of her moving to one of the chairs, and it wasn't difficult to imagine her hesitance and wariness as she sat down. He knew this wasn't what she'd planned, just as her bombshell hadn't been on the cards for him. He'd looked forward to resuming what they'd had but she'd aimed to lob her hand grenade and then disappear once the deed had been done, with consequences to be dealt with at a later date.

'Great. Thank you. The bed was very comfortable.'

Leo turned, brought her some coffee and went through the business of asking her what she wanted to eat. He'd been here off and on over the years but it was a first for him to have a woman in here with him. For him, the villa was a sanctuary from the pace of life he led. He could have afforded to have help—a housekeeper, a chef, whatever the hell he wanted—but he had always chosen not to. He liked the uncluttered business of not having anyone around. He enjoyed the solitude of losing himself in the peace and calm the island afforded.

However, the down side was that now, in

these awkward, challenging circumstances, there was no one to break the intimacy between them—because there *was* intimacy. How could there not be?

Whether she cared to admit it or not, they'd been lovers. He'd touched her everywhere, just as she had touched him. Her head might insist on forgetting that little technicality but her body would certainly remember every second of what they'd shared. It had remembered fast enough last night, just something else she wanted to pretend had never happened.

How could she not see all the advantages of the arrangement he had put on the table? How could she not appreciate the importance of providing stability for the child they had created together? It wasn't as though they didn't get along. It wasn't as though they weren't still hot for one another.

Why couldn't she see how superfluous the business of *love* was? That abstract dream that people always seemed to insist on chasing, even though reality always ended up stepping in to remind them that it was a chimera.

How could she not see that all he wanted was for his offspring to have the sort of family life he'd never had? And it would be a good life. No way was he going to let her disappear without some delaying tactics… If he had to buy time, then that was what he was going to do.

They ate a breakfast of local, buttery bread with cheese and fresh orange juice.

Kaya cleared her throat when the last of the breakfast had been eaten. 'I guess we should have this conversation about the way forward you talked about.'

'Not yet.'

'But…'

'Like I said, I want to show you the island. It's hot now. It's going to get hotter still. It'll be pleasant being outside. Did you bring a swim-suit?'

'No!'

'No problem. There are some pretty good shops in the town.'

'Leo, I don't plan on staying long enough to get in the sea.'

Leo shrugged and decided that with a little persuasion she might find herself changing her mind. Dark eyes briefly rested on her with brooding intensity, and he saw the slow curl of colour that spread into her cheeks and the way her eyes skittered away. He noted the jumpiness of a woman who still wanted to touch him, was still attracted to him. She'd eventually pulled back, the evening before when he'd touched her, but only eventually.

'We can spend the day out, have a look around...visit a couple of the beaches. This place is known for its pink sands—something to do with tiny organisms that attach to the coral in the sea. And of course for its architecture— very New England, but with a backdrop of palm trees and flowers you'd never get in New England itself. You'll like it. Have you ever been to this part of the world?'

'Leo...'

'Trust me, there won't be any pressure from me for you to revisit my proposal. This is just an attempt for us to discuss the situation as... friends.'

'Friends...'

'Exactly. You have to admit, we haven't had a problem getting along. Why adopt a hostile stance because of what's happened? Much better to approach this situation amicably.'

'Okay...'

'Excellent!' He dumped the dishes in the sink and then remained there, leaning against the counter with his arms folded. 'I have a couple of things to do on the work front. Should take about an hour. Explore the grounds! And... I'll meet you by the front door in an hour and a half?'

Kaya nodded.

She had the weirdest feeling that she was suddenly trying to balance on quicksand, although she had to admit that he was being as charming, fair and gentlemanly about the whole thing than she could ever have hoped. Even after she'd fallen into his arms the evening before, like a starving person in the presence of food, he had remained amicable and fair and hadn't reminded her of her temporary weakness.

Because he was essentially a great guy... Why else had she fallen for him?

Which made her think of those women who would soon be auditioning for the role of wife.

It was an uneasy thought, and she pushed it away and blinked as he walked her to the kitchen door, smiling and turning down her offer to tidy the kitchen since he had work to do, and instead ushering her to the French doors at the back which led out to the gardens she had enjoyed earlier from her bedroom window.

And then she was left on her own.

'If you need me—' he pointed to a vague point away from the kitchen to the side '—the room I use as my office is there. Feel free to disturb me.'

Then he'd smiled that crooked, sexy smile that did crazy things to her body and headed off, leaving her to her own devices.

Off to start cutting and pasting adverts for a suitable wife, Kaya thought sourly. She'd noticed that marriage chat had hit the buffers. He certainly hadn't spent long pursuing that line.

She explored the grounds and just about managed to cling on to her determination to be detached about what was happening and not be swayed by seductive talk about marriage. There was a pool to the side. It was cleverly done to blend in with the tropical scenery, and at first glance almost seemed to be part of the landscape with its rich overhang of trees, and a rock pool set at just the right height to tumble as a small waterfall into the turquoise depths.

With the sun getting higher and hotter, Kaya longed to dive in. Instead, she took her time exploring everywhere. The enormous lawns with little clusters of seating here and there under shady trees, and then that tantalising glimpse of sea and the faint rumble of waves.

Leo was waiting for her when, at the appointed time, she headed for the front door, much hotter than she had been an hour and a half previously.

He was wearing loafers and looked cool and relaxed, hands shoved into the pockets of loose, cotton trousers and the same tee-shirt he had been wearing earlier.

'You look hot,' was the first thing he murmured as he ushered her through the front door and towards a small four-wheel drive which she hadn't noticed when she'd first arrived. His hand, lightly resting on the small of her back, made her feel even hotter than she already was.

'I...' She ducked quickly into the passenger seat and smoothed her dress down as she waited for him to join her. 'I hadn't realised how hot it would be here. A different kind of heat to summers at home.'

'Yes,' Leo agreed gravely, eyeing her dress, which was sticking to her like glue. 'The heat is a lot less polite over here, although it's alleviated by the ocean breezes. You'll find that when we're at the beach. I've arranged a boat so I can take you away from the main drag to one of the quieter coves only accessible by sea.'

'Have you?'

'Why not?' He glanced sideways at her, making sure to roll the windows up and switch on the air conditioning for her benefit, even though he would have preferred the wind blowing through. 'Like you said, you're in a hurry to head back and, if we're going to have the conversation we need to have, then having it somewhere a little more private than a busy beach makes sense. I've also arranged a picnic for us to take. Food is of the essence, wouldn't you agree, in your condition?'

'I wouldn't say of the *essence*,' Kaya returned

faintly as the little car gave a full-throttle growl and kicked into life.

Leo's voice was quiet and serious. 'One thing you've got to understand is, whatever decision is made about this situation, the welfare of our baby is paramount to me. Skipping meals isn't a good idea—nor is over-heating. You look very hot in that dress. Have you got a hat? Something to keep the sun off your face?'

'Leo, I'm not an invalid! I'm pregnant!'

'All the same...' Leo murmured.

Kaya didn't say anything. She hadn't really banked on this level of solicitousness and it made her feel a little guilty. Had she over-simplified what his reaction would be? She'd known that he would never walk away from his responsibility, but she had balanced that against his lack of interest in permanence and the fact that he didn't love her, that they had already broken up.

She hadn't foreseen how passionate and blinkered his reaction would be, and yet why not? How could she not have predicted that his sense of responsibility might actually be *enhanced* by the fact that he had always blamed his own abandonment on irresponsible parents? That story might not have changed with the discovery of Julie Anne's journal.

And how would that feed into a need to create the perfect family unit, the very one he had not had? With or without her.

He was showing, even at this early stage, all the signs of being the perfect father. He was a guy who gave one hundred percent. Would he be the guy who gave one hundred percent to the married life he'd never planned to have? One hundred percent to a woman who wouldn't demand love, romance and promises of a perfect life, but would be more than happy to wear his ring and enjoy all the material advantages that came with it? Like this villa in the Bahamas, for starters.

She looked at the splendid scenery around them as he drove. Swaying coconut trees sprinkled along the coastline; the sky was the colour of purest aquamarine; flowers, bushes, shrubs and foliage bordered the tarmac in Technicolor disarray. And then she fell silent as they entered the town and she saw what he'd meant about the architecture.

The houses were sparkling bright, a million shades of ice-cream pastels, and the neat fences bordering them in perfect formation were diamond-white, gleaming under the sun. The shops, the cafés and the little boutiques were all picture-perfect against the backdrop of palm trees and flowers, and the place was bustling with locals and tourists.

He swerved into a parking space and flung open his door and, when she looked at him in bewilderment, he gently reminded her, 'Picnic, remember? I have to collect it before we go get the boat and...' He gave her a friendly once-over. 'Your dress... The trainers... Let's get you some more appropriate clothes.'

'No! I'm fine!'

'Shorts...a swimsuit...flip flops...'

He refused to take no for an answer. He described what she needed in words that made her long for the coolness of a dress that wasn't sticking to her, and trainers that weren't making her feet sweat.

He held her hand in a helpful, brotherly manner that made her teeth snap together, even though she couldn't take issue with him, and it wasn't his fault that he'd planted ideas in her head that wouldn't go away.

The sun poured down like honey and going into each air-conditioned shop was bliss. She barely noticed the things he was buying for her.

'You'll have to get used to this while you're carrying my child,' he murmured when she protested at purchase number one. 'It's important you're comfortable, and you're not going to be comfortable in what you're wearing.'

'And what after the baby's born?' Kaya asked.

'Well,' Leo murmured coolly, leaning into

her so that there was no missing the relevance of what he was saying. 'Naturally, you will be taken care of as the mother of my child. What you choose to do with that money will be entirely up to you. It will, however, be a slightly different matter should you become involved with another man and choose to marry.'

In the act of feeling the soft silk of a sarong, Kaya paused and looked at him.

'You mean…?'

'I mean my child will have everything within my power to give but…and call me old-fashioned…if you meet another man and get married, then it will be up to him to look after you. I would want to see where my money goes— make sure it's going to my child and not feathering another man's nest. This will all be legally sorted.'

He stood back and smiled, and in that moment, Kaya knew that ground rules were being laid down and that the conversation they needed to have, however jolly the atmosphere he was trying to create, had begun.

He was scrupulously fair, and would be incredibly generous, but he was warning her of boundary lines and he would stick to those.

The road she decided to travel down would have consequences and she would have to accept that.

'I would never take money from you to…' Her voice trailed off.

'I know.' Leo soothed her, his voice relaxing into a smile, resetting the tempo of the day. 'But I've never been a man to take unnecessary chances…'

CHAPTER NINE

LEO COULD TELL that the effect of what he had said had made Kaya stop and think. But wasn't that fair enough? He wasn't being unreasonable. He was simply saying it as it was. She wanted to sally forth in search of true love, and that was fine, but there was no way he was going to let her grow into the notion that his money would go towards supporting another man. Indeed, the thought of it made him clench his fists in impotent fury.

She was his woman.

Leo wasn't sure when this idea had taken root, but he didn't question it, because she was pregnant with *his* child. How could it be otherwise?

Competition was staring Leo in the face and it enraged him. A mythical guy yet to appear on the scene… The more he thought about this faceless person, the more determined he was to eliminate the threat.

He'd planted seeds that had to be planted. He had let her know, in no uncertain terms, that what was good for the goose was also good for the gander. If she wanted to pursue love and find the perfect partner, then he would likewise engage in a pursuit of his own. Not love, but suitability. The net result would be the same— a partner.

If she refused to buy into the only sensible solution to the situation, then she would have to think long and hard about what happened next.

In the meantime, while she was captive on this beautiful island, and without forcing her hand at all, he intended to use every trick in the book to persuade her to see things from his point of view and to accept that there were far more important things in life than the airy-fairy nonsense of *love*.

He had started with the matter-of-fact realities of life for them both as their ways diverged, leaving only the child they had created as the common link.

Would she be able to contemplate another woman having fun with their son or daughter any more easily than he could contemplate another man sharing what would not be theirs to share?

She would have time to think about that one. Meanwhile…

'There's a lot more to see of the town,' he said, waiting until she had belted up before starting.

They had detoured to collect their picnic from one of the upmarket restaurants. It was beautifully arranged in a wicker hamper, with a cooler box full of various drinks. He dumped it in the boot along with the towels he had brought and the oversized rug to put down on the sand.

When they made it to the cove she would be left speechless and impressed. It was all part of the lifestyle that could be hers, should she so choose. A little quiet temptation could do no harm.

He slid a sideways glance at her. No one could say that he wasn't enjoying the moment, whatever the gravity of the circumstances.

She had changed out of the dress and trainers into some loose shorts and flip-flops, and a delicious expanse of silky-smooth, golden-brown legs was on display. The top was small and loose yet managed to be incredibly sexy.

It was all too easy to recall the feel of that slender body under him: the high, small breasts with their succulent brown nipples; the flat, smooth belly; the jut of her hips and the grind of her body… It was all too easy to remember the taste of her when he had explored every inch of her, taking his time.

And all too easy to think about them being together again, bodies merging, finding pleasure in what had come so naturally.

He could show her that they could be good together. There was nothing wrong in doing that. He could show her that he could be a good father, a thoughtful partner...and an ardent lover.

He could show her that there was no such thing as the *perfect* life but there was such a thing as a perfectly *acceptable* life.

'What I've seen is lovely,' Kaya returned politely.

The car windows were open, at her insistence, and she had tied her hair back. There was a large straw hat for her to wear to protect her from the midday sun when they got to wherever they were going, even though, as she had reminded him, she wasn't a pale blonde who went red at the first hint of heat.

But he had insisted. She had never known anyone be so solicitous with a pregnant partner. It felt good to be looked after. It made her think that she had become too accustomed to being the one who did the looking after and not the other way round, even when her mother no longer needed care-taking. Old habits died hard.

She shivered when she thought that all that instinct to protect would go to another woman in due course. But time and again she returned to the misery of a life without love, a life in which responsibility became the driving force with the heartache of knowing that, one day, that responsibility would dim and everything would end up crashing and burning.

Was she being too fussy?

She glanced surreptitiously at his strong, tanned thighs and the strong forearms on the steering wheel, and then had a quick drink of his profile and the way the wind blew back his slightly long, dark hair.

They reached the marina and a boat was waiting for them, small and white with a bright-red canvas roof. The motor was an outboard old-fashioned one and an old guy in shorts and a vest was doing a balancing act as the little boat bobbed on the water.

Around them, the promenade was busy with people coming and going. Cafés, with bright-blue-and-red umbrellas sheltering busy outdoor tables, gave people having lunch and drinks a perfect view of the ocean.

Kaya didn't have to look round to know that somebody was bringing all the gear from the car to the boat, jumping to the command of some invisible signal Leo seemed to give. She was starting to understand that, the minute cash was waved, all things became possible.

Leo was taking charge. When he held out his

hand to help her into the gently bobbing boat, steadying her as she tottered on, she felt stupidly feminine.

'Okay?'

She nodded as he leant into her, and then they were off, buzzing away from the jetty where the boat had been docked, moving at a snail's pace. Oh, how blissful it was.

There were just so many things she'd never done! Lying back on a small boat putt-putting across turquoise seas, with the wind in her hair and her thoughts too lazy to do much, was one of those.

And she loved it.

From her vantage point she could appreciate the strong, muscular lines of Leo's body. He had shoved on some ultra-dark sunglasses and he looked every inch the guy people had probably once thought would never amount to much. Trapped in care but too smart, too aggressive and too tenacious ever to be kept down.

Was it any wonder she'd fallen for him?

Leo, glancing back over his shoulder, steering with one hand on the tiller, caught an expression on Kaya's face that struck up in him, a lazy, assessing watchfulness that spoke volumes.

Lounging back on the wooden plank seat of the very basic boat, she was as elegant as an old-fashioned Hollywood movie star, but without the artifice. He wondered whether she thought that the straw hat was blocking her expression, and he hoped she did, because he was enjoying that lazy, lingering look on her face.

He tipped up the sunglasses, noted the way she tried to revert back to the stern, no-nonsense expression she had been cultivating ever since she had arrived and felt a wave of quiet satisfaction She was no more immune to him than he was to her.

'Look over there.' He nodded to a point slightly behind her and she duly turned. 'That's the cove.'

'Wow.'

Leo watched with darkly appreciative eyes as she hoisted herself into an upright position, twisting and holding on to the hat with both hands, drinking in what could only be called absolute tropical perfection.

They had left the crowds behind and had reached the cove, which was utterly private, a huddled bank of pale-pink sand nestled amidst a backdrop of dense foliage, bush and coconut trees. The water rippling up to the shore was so clear that the dart of little silver fish swimming in small schools could be seen, swerving hither and thither.

He anchored the boat, killed the engine and

for a moment took in the magnificent scenery, just as Kaya did.

He joined her on the bench and she felt the unsteady dip of the boat under the weight transfer.

'I've only been to this cove a handful of times,' he admitted.

'You're mad.' Kaya turned to find him closer to her than she'd expected, his thighs lightly brushing hers. 'If I had a house on this island, I'd be here every day.'

'That would prove tricky on the work front.' Leo smiled drily, his expression once again hidden behind his sunglasses. 'The Internet connection is non-existent.'

'Still…'

'Have you decided what you'll do when you get back to Canada?'

Kaya licked her lips. She didn't want to think about that but wasn't that why they were here—to discuss the future quietly in a private spot, like two adults about to part ways and head down different roads?

'You *have* remembered that that's why we're here, haven't you?' Leo stood up, balanced and began shoving the stuff they'd brought with them to the side, leaving her to fulminate over his question, to confront her choices.

Staring, Kaya remained open-mouthed for a

few seconds then she scrambled behind him, nearly losing her balance. Her heart was racing, and racing even more when he helped her out of the boat into shallow, clear water that was beautifully warm. She had bought a swimsuit and was wearing it under the shorts, an unadventurous black affair that anyone's granny would have been proud to wear.

Had all this frivolous clothes-buying, picnic-gathering and tourist-gawping somehow made her forget the point of her being here in the first place? What had happened to her determination to stay just long enough to break the news face-to-face, before returning to Canada to sort herself out and move on with her new life?

'Of course I've thought about it,' she informed him just as soon as they were both on land and he had heaved their belongings out of the boat, which was now rocking gently to one side while they set up camp further along under the semi-shade of overhanging trees.

'Good!'

Kaya smiled tightly. She watched in silence as he spread the rug, handed her a towel and then stripped down to his swimming trunks, at which point her mouth went dry.

'You should get out of the shorts, Kaya. It's too hot to have anything on but a swimsuit, and

I take it you *are* going to go into the sea, aren't you? There's nothing like it, trust me.'

'I will in a minute,' she muttered. She didn't want those dark eyes in her direction, looking at her from behind dark sunglasses, making her feel hot and bothered and reminding her of what she wanted from him but couldn't have. She didn't want her body misbehaving...*again*.

'We need to discuss the business of where you'll live,' Leo murmured, filling the silence.

'What do you mean?'

'I live in Manhattan. Yes, I'm willing to commute, especially in the early stages—possibly buy somewhere in Vancouver as a base—but realistically that wouldn't be a long-term solution.'

'What are you suggesting?'

'You know where I'm going with this.' Leo didn't bother pulling his punches. 'This situation is going to require sacrifices and that's where we're going to have to meet in the middle.'

'I've never lived anywhere but Canada...and of course Alaska, when I was very young, but that doesn't count, not really.'

'Times change. I think twenty miles' distance from one another should do it, don't you agree? I have an office in Boston and would consider relocating there. There are many attractive places in and around that part of the world that will allow joint custody to work very well between us.'

'Joint custody…'

'It *is* what you're after, isn't it? You don't want marriage, so that will have to be the next option.'

'Of course. Yes, that's exactly what I want.'

'Splendid. We can informally agree that, until he or she is one, I will take the brunt of the sacrifice on my shoulders and travel as necessary. We can revisit that arrangement at that point. As far as visiting rights are concerned, nothing has to be put on paper at the beginning, as far as I'm concerned, although that will be open to change.'

'I don't understand…'

'If at some point sticking to a regular, agreed schedule becomes difficult, then naturally lawyers will be involved.'

Kaya paled at the vision being painted in front of her although he made sense. Compromises would have to be made; a life of sharing timetables would have to be worked out.

'In the meantime—' he waved one hand to smooth over the temporary tension '—I will have my PA sort out alternative, suitable accommodation for you wherever you agree to settle. A relocation company would probably work best, and naturally money would be no object. You just need to tell me what sort of place you're after. You can leave the rest to me. A shortlist will be compiled to save you the trouble of taking too many long-distance trips when you'd be better off...getting your affairs in order and, of course, resting.'

'This all feels as though it's moving very fast,' Kaya said a little unsteadily. 'I'm not even three months' pregnant yet!'

Leo looked at her, unsmiling, propping himself up on one hand and removing the sunglasses to stare at her. 'There's a lot to sort out,' he told her, pausing for her to digest that and join the dots to the alternative, which would have been painfully simple in comparison. Joint custody and finding separate properties would not have been a necessary consideration, for starters. 'I don't think that sticking our heads in the sand and waiting until the last minute is going to work, do you?'

'No, but...'

'We can continue this later,' Leo drawled, throwing her a lifebelt, leaving her to mull over what he had said. 'Right now, I'm going to take a dip. Join me?'

'I... Perhaps in a minute...'

Leo shrugged and stood up, a thing of masculine beauty, every muscle honed to perfection. Kaya followed him with her eyes as he strolled down to the sea, waded in and then took the plunge to slice through the blue, blue water, his movements smooth, fast and confident.

Leo disappearing into the distance felt like a telling pointer to the role he would eventually adopt in her life. Someone moving away from her, vanishing to new horizons with someone else but always, painfully, returning because of the child they shared. Always returning to shore but never to be with her in any significant way.

And thinking about that hurt.

She sneakily stripped down to the one-piece and, after a while, when over-heating seemed to be a threat, she headed out to sea.

She had been brought up in snow and was an excellent skier. She loved that wonderful freedom but the confidence she had hurtling down a snowy slope was lacking when it came to water. She'd learnt to swim as an adult, sporadic lessons here and there, teaching her just enough to be safe.

She tentatively waded out. Leo was a speck in the faraway distance. He was lying on his back staring up at the sky, not a care in the world, from the looks of it. Whereas she...felt as though she had been assailed from every possible angle by a bombardment of realities and truths she hadn't banked on.

She had naively come out here to do the decent thing and tell him about the pregnancy face-to-face, expecting to be the one to drop the bomb, the one in ultimate control. She'd had the situation clear in her head. Leo didn't love her and, however decent he was, he had never been interested in a relationship. She'd thought she would be doing them both a favour by giving him options and walking away to let him consider them. So how come she was the one floundering now?

Wrapped up in her thoughts, and becoming increasingly confident in the warm, clear, shallow water, Kaya wasn't expecting the tiny drop in the ocean floor, a shifting of the sand between her toes, and she gave a panicked yelp as she lost her footing.

Fear of drowning overcame the voice in her head telling her that this was not a dangerous situation. Panic made her splash and flounder, surfacing and gasping.

She was choking and gasping, and barely noticed Leo moving as fast as a shark in her direction until she felt his arms around her. She clung and practically sobbed her relief.

'Jesus, Kaya!'

For once, her usual fiery independence deserted her. She was just so grateful to feel safe as he carried her back to shore and laid her on the rug as gently as if she were a piece of porcelain.

'I panicked. I feel like a fool. Thank goodness there's no one here! I... I'm sorry.'

'Why are you apologising?' Leo said roughly. 'You scared the hell out of me.'

'I'm not a strong swimmer,' she confessed in a sheepish whisper. 'I never had lessons when I was a kid and then, as an adult, well, it's different. I can keep myself above water but that's about it. The bank suddenly dropped and I... I panicked and couldn't think straight.'

She drank some water and looked at him, ensnared by his eyes, and she realised in a heartbeat that this was what she would blithely be giving up—this safety with a guy who would always look out for her. Maybe not because he loved her, maybe just because of their child, but she would be safe with him. Her heart might not be safe, but everything else would be, because he would be the guy she could always count on.

Feeling *safe* was a luxury she had not always been able to count on. Her young, grieving and distracted mother had loved her, and had been fun, but when it had come to providing a safety net... For a long time she had been simply too selfish to pick up that baton.

'Understandable,' Leo murmured.

'What would I have done if you hadn't swum

to my rescue?' She shivered when she thought about how cavalier she had been, going into the sea when she was a timid swimmer, when she was *pregnant*, had another *life* to consider...

And then she thought about how cavalier she was being now, waving aside Leo's marriage proposal and everything that came with it, waving aside the security of a united family for the sake of her own self-protection.

If things got truly unbearable wouldn't divorce always be a possibility? Wasn't it worth trying, at the very least?

'You wouldn't have been here in the first place,' Leo pointed out reasonably.

'Thank you.' She smiled.

'For coming to your rescue? You wouldn't have drowned, Kaya. I guarantee that. The drop may have been sudden enough to freak you out but you would have recovered. Nothing would have been lost but a little of your self-aplomb.' He stroked back her wet hair.

In return Kaya hesitantly touched his cheek and felt him still under her hand. His eyes darkened with just the hint of the obvious question in their depths.

'Okay,' she said quietly.

'Okay? What does *okay* mean?'

He'd stepped back, not trying to force her hand, respecting her decision...waiting for her to come to him. Was that what was happening now? Was she coming to him? He was giddy with relief at the thought of that.

He'd swum out there, enjoying the cool peace of the ocean around him, and he'd lain on his back, gently floating and mentally trying to work out whether he'd done the right thing in not pushing her.

It made him sick when he thought about how much was at stake. From never having contemplated the prospect of being a father, he'd been catapulted into a possessiveness that had knocked him for six. He'd gone from the guy who had complete control over every aspect of his life to the guy who had none in these new, unforeseen circumstances.

He'd missed her. He'd never missed anyone in his life before but he'd missed her when he'd returned to New York. He'd ached for her and now, with so much at stake, he could scarcely breathe for expectation.

Inside, emotions swirled, things he'd never felt before just out of reach. He felt vulnerable and bewildered at the same time and keen to find some solid ground.

He had had to grit his teeth to hold on to his game plan but the feel of her hand on his cheek felt almost too good to be true.

If he were to think of this in terms of winning and losing, had he *won*? *Had his patience paid off*? He could think like this. It was easier than getting lost in stuff he didn't understand, in feelings that made him edgy, impatient and nervous.

'Okay,' he quipped unsteadily, 'You believe me when I tell you that drowning was never going to happen?'

'Okay, I'll marry you.' Kaya inhaled deeply, well aware of the enormity of her decision, but determined to pull back from the temptation to let go of all her pride. 'For all the reasons you say, it makes sense.'

'What about love?' Leo asked with a shuttered expression. 'What about your dreams of finding Mr Perfect?'

Kaya lowered her eyes. 'Sometimes it's important to think of the bigger picture.'

Was that the non-answer he was looking for? He was getting what he wanted—a marriage that was necessary, as far as he was concerned, given the circumstances—and yet something inside him twisted because he suddenly wanted more than concerns about the bigger picture.

Still, the main thing was that he was getting what he wanted. She'd made her decision, and it wasn't as though he had levered threats or tried to use his wealth to bribe her into doing what he wanted, what he knew was the only thing to do.

'Look on the bright side,' he murmured, capturing her hand with his and planting a gentle kiss on her wrist, his dark eyes never leaving hers. 'We still have *this*.'

Kaya didn't pretend to misunderstand. Her body agreed with every word of that. They might not have *love*, he was saying, but they had sex.

It would have to do.

She would enjoy it—and what was ever perfect in life, when she thought about it?

She drew him towards her and felt liberated. He kissed her, a gentle, enquiring kiss, a kiss that still tiptoed around the decision she had made. She pulled him into her so that they toppled back, half-laughing, her mouth never leaving his.

No turning back.

They made love surrounded by the sea, the surf and the blue skies above, just the two of them here in this wonderful bubble. For her, it was wonderful, passionate, bitter-sweet love. She enjoyed him in the knowledge that this was all there could ever be and it was going to have to be enough.

'What if someone comes?' she whispered as he slowly tugged down the swimsuit top to expose her breasts. He grinned and propped himself up on his hands to stare down at her.

'No chance. The island is very private, and if anyone approaches by boat we would hear from a distance away. But, trust me, that's not going to happen. What's going to happen, my darling, is this…'

Kaya melted into the tenderness of his love-making. He was the ultimate thoughtful lover, respectful of her pregnancy, even though she told him that there was no need to be. But secretly she adored that respect, adored the way he made her feel, as though she was the most delicate thing on the planet and to be protected at all costs, even when it came to over-frisky love-making.

He suckled on her breasts, cupped them in his hands and told her that he could already feel that they were fuller, riper, her nipples bigger and darker.

'And more sensitive,' Kaya murmured, lying back with shameless abandon as she urged him to suck harder until she was sure she could come just from the wet caress of his mouth on her nipples.

He stripped her and it was glorious, feeling the warm sun on her body and the soft sand between her toes when her feet slid away from the rug.

His erection, freed from the swimming trunks, told her all there was to know, that this man still very much wanted her, but she'd known that all along.

He parted her legs and the breath hitched in her throat as he played with her there, teasing her with his fingers, mouth and tongue, finding her clitoris and stimulating it until she was writhing with pleasure.

She begged him to stop, and begged him not to stop, which made him smile. She was open and ready for him when at last he thrust into her, long and deep, and moving with gentle, persistent rhythm.

He pushed a little deeper every time until she was shuddering into exquisite orgasm, shaking and trembling as she climbed higher and higher, and her fingers clutched and dug into his tightly corded shoulder blades.

Sated, Kaya lay against him and felt complete.

She knew that she would always have to be careful, to make sure that the love she felt wasn't reflected in her face. What would happen if she told him that she'd fallen in love with him? Right now, with no ring on her finger, he would back off. She knew he would. But later, if they were married? Something would be lost. The easy familiarity of friendship which he was willing to extend would seep away, replaced with awkwardness and discomfort until whatever they had, from lust to affection, would wither and die.

She couldn't bear the thought of that.

But what she was signing up to? However tough it felt would be a lot less tough than the alternative, and she basked in that realisation and smiled at him.

'I've missed you,' Leo confessed in a roughened undertone. He stroked back her hair and smiled down at her.

You've missed this, Kaya thought realistically.

'So,' she said softly. 'I guess plans need to be revisited?'

'We can revisit them after we've had a swim, and this time I'm going to be right by your side, so you have nothing to fear. Then we're going to have a long, lazy lunch, and then maybe we can have a bit more fun... And when we're back at the villa we can do the revisiting...'

'Okay.' She began getting to her feet and he gently tugged her back down and tilted her so that they were looking at one another, their faces only inches apart.

Kaya could see every laughter line on his face, every worry line. His dark eyes were deadly serious.

'Sure about this?'

Kaya nodded.

'You were right.' She sighed with heartfelt

sincerity. 'We're bringing a child into the world. That child didn't ask to be here but it's important that we both do what's right for him or her. And putting aside…well, the stuff I'd hoped for when it came to marriage and kids…is just something that has to be done.'

She was only saying what he had said to her in the first place. She'd come round to his way of thinking. The *responsible* way of thinking.

'Kaya,' he said huskily, 'I…'

I love you? Leo froze. He didn't know where that had come from. He couldn't love her. He couldn't *love*. His heart thudded, protesting that assumption.

'You what…?'

'You're doing the right thing.'

Love? He found it hard to think straight and he knew he had to get past this crazy nonsense and focus on the here and now. She was going to marry him. They were doing the thing that made sense, the thing that was best for their child. Children didn't ask to be born and should never have to pay the price for mistakes their parents had made.

They would have that thought guiding them and they would have sex. The physical side of things, he could understand, and that thought calmed him.

'I'm just doing what you're doing, Leo. I'm

making sacrifices. You're prepared to move to Boston and I know that'll probably be a huge wrench for you.'

The sun was beating down on them and the rug felt hot, even under the shade of the tree with its low-hanging branches.

The sound of the sea, gentle against the shore, was soporific.

Leo stared into her eyes and had trouble swallowing. She was everything to him. He was the sacrifice she was forced to make. Sex and a baby would be their bond.

He'd lived his life with sex as the only thing he could offer a woman but, now he wanted to offer so much more, he was with a woman who wanted it all but from another man.

She would give everything up, including the place she called home, so that she could do the right thing. And that was what he had persuaded her to do by presenting her with facts, figures and scenarios that he'd known would unsettle her. He'd set his mind on something and had used every trick in the book to get what he'd wanted.

He hadn't bothered to dig deeper into things that should have unsettled *him*: why he'd missed her so much; why his heart turned over when he thought of her; why spending the rest of his life with her had been a decision he'd reached without batting an eye, baby or no baby.

She was talking about Boston, building herself up to a move, and sounding cheerful about it.

He interrupted her mid-sentence. He could take what she was offering, touch her soft mouth, make love to her and feel her body moulding to hers.

'Kaya…'

She smiled but his eyes were grave when he looked at her.

'This time, it's for me to apologise. It's not going to work.'

'What?' She was still smiling.

'Marriage. You were right—it's not for us. Boston, yes, that makes sense. But marriage? No. We have to let that one go.'

CHAPTER TEN

BOSTON…MARRIAGE…THE sort of picture-perfect gingerbread cottage he had always scorned: *that* was what was on Leo's mind ten days later as he stared out of the vast expanse of glass that separated him from the busy Manhattan streets below.

He could have had it all. He could have had the woman he'd fallen in love with. He could have just accepted that the circumstances weren't ideal and he was now plagued by what he had given up.

If things had been bad for him before he'd gone to his villa in the Bahamas, then they were indescribable now. He ached from the sorrow of knowing what he couldn't have and from the vague notion that he had brought the whole situation about all by himself.

He'd been arrogant and smug. He had slept with Kaya and managed to convince himself that he was untouchable because he always had been. He'd known the kind of guy she wanted but, instead of showing her from the start that he was that guy, when he scraped away the superficial stuff he had glibly shrugged and assumed that the sort of considerate man she was after, the sort of man who made dreams come true for women and wanted a future with them, wasn't him.

He hadn't spotted love for what it was until it was too late. He couldn't blame himself for that but he did blame himself for misreading the signposts along the way.

Now she was gone. Not to Boston, not to house-hunt with him, even though he had done his best to try and convince her to, but back to Vancouver to think things through.

He hadn't had a leg to stand on so he had been forced to let her go. The last day they'd spent in the Bahamas had been agony for him but he had concealed it well.

And her? She had carried on smiling, not once berating him for stringing her along, and not once implying that she had known best all along. She had been sweet, quiet and well-mannered and, in return, he'd backed away and fought against the pain of watching her and seeing her leave him.

He had no idea what she was thinking about Boston. If she decided to stay put in Vancouver, then there wasn't a thing he could do about it. He couldn't drag her kicking and screaming to some house he'd chosen for her.

And he'd been looking. It was a job he could have farmed out to his PA, but he had spent time looking himself, getting in touch with the biggest relocation company that dealt with that area and outlining the sort of thing he was looking for.

He looked at his mobile phone and, fed up with the business of dealing with his chaotic thoughts, he scrolled, found her number and dialled it.

Kaya was tidying the last of the rooms in the house. It had been a labour of love and a useful way of getting her mind off what was happening in her life.

So he'd changed his mind about marrying her. Was it that surprising? Maybe he'd made love with her that last time and it had dawned on him that sex, for what it was worth, wasn't going to be quite enough to see them through a baby and everything that would come afterwards.

He'd broken it off, she'd looked at him while her world had been falling apart and she'd smiled and kept on smiling, nodding her agreement with his decision for the rest of the short time they'd been at the villa.

She was sure he'd been relieved that she'd had the decency not to kick up a fuss or to tell him that he should have listened to her in the first place. It was hard to tell. When he chose, it was impossible to read what he was thinking.

And, once she'd returned to the house, he had called daily to find out how she was doing. He was solicitous and zealous in his concern for her health, the pregnancy. He asked her questions and she replied, but all the while she wondered what he was doing, what he was getting up to.

Out of sight, out of mind—wasn't that how it went? He'd walked away from her and was living his life as it had been before they'd met. Had he met someone else? Someone to take the sting out of the hand he'd been dealt? Had he idly started casting his eyes around for the women who would step up to the plate, expecting no more than he considered himself capable of giving?

He'd mentioned Boston.

When Kaya thought of going there, of looking around houses knowing that she wouldn't be sharing any of them with him, she chickened out and made excuses for not being ready.

'Still stuff to do here...'

'I have to go to the halfway house and go through the books...'

'I can't spare the time right now to go to the

estate agents… Maybe later, maybe next week… or next month…'

'Is there really a rush just yet…?'

Now, sitting back on her haunches with little piles of paraphernalia around her, and the growing emptiness of the house reminding her that decisions couldn't be put off for ever, she looked at her phone and saw his name. He could have phoned her on the hour and, every single time his name flashed up, she'd know that her heart would skip a beat.

'Leo, hi.'

What was she doing…? How much left was there to pack away…? Did she need any assistance? He could have a team assembled within a day to finish everything off for her… She shouldn't be doing anything that required manual effort, not in her condition; it was important she took care of herself…

Kaya stared off into the distance as she heard the dark, velvety smoothness of his voice and listened to his concern, always at the forefront, always reminding her of the kind of guy he was, so much the opposite of what she had originally thought.

'It's good for me, doing this,' she said quietly. 'It's a lot of personal stuff. It wouldn't feel right for a team of people to be here going through it.'

'I get that, but you're pregnant.'

'You worry too much. I'm fine. I… Leo… about Boston…'

'It's actually why I was calling you.'

Down the end of the line, Leo vaulted to his feet and strolled to the bank of windows that overlooked Wall Street. He was going to pin her down. A decision had to be made. His head was exploding from not knowing, from her being so far from him, her voice so distant down the end of an impersonal line.

'I've been working on this and I've found somewhere I think would be suitable.'

'Really? For me, Leo? How do you know what I would find suitable?'

'I'm going on instinct and, as you don't seem that interested in finding anywhere there, it's all I have to go on.'

'I'm sorry. There's been a lot to do here, with the house and everything.'

'Granted, but time won't be standing still.'

'Maybe you could email me the details and I'll let you know what I think of the place, you know? Save all the bother of travelling from Vancouver to Boston.'

Leo gritted his teeth at her airy dismissal.

She couldn't have made it more obvious that the last thing she wanted was to see him. Unfortunately, the more he thought about it—and he'd spent most of the past couple of weeks doing nothing *but* thinking about it—the more his gut told him that, the longer she remained holed up in Vancouver, the less likely it would be that she would consider moving location to fit in with what he wanted.

She would find her comfort zone, the place where she felt she belonged, she would eventually just refuse point-blank to accommodate him and there would be nothing he could do about it.

'You'll be chauffeur-driven to my private jet and met at the airstrip by my PA, Kaya. Trust me, there won't be any bother.'

'Your PA…'

'Would you rather she show you around with the estate agent?' It was a job keeping the edge out of his voice. He couldn't bear the thought of her not wanting to see him. He hated to think that she was toughening up, getting used to not having him anywhere in her life.

'It might be a good idea.' Her voice was cool and reasonable. 'If I have to see a bunch of houses, then I wouldn't want to waste your time by dragging you out every time one comes up on the market. That okay?'

'Fine,' Leo said through gritted teeth, thinking that it was absolutely in no way *okay*. 'No problem at all.'

Kaya was sitting in his private jet less than a day and a half later. She barely noticed the luxury, its leather and walnut perfection. She had

had details of her trip texted to her and had realised that she couldn't keep dodging the inevitable for ever.

If she'd wanted to, she could have stayed in Vancouver, made him tailor his busy life to suit her, but that would have been petty and spiteful. The truth was that, as Julie Anne's house had started emptying, its soul had begun to disappear and, as it had disappeared, the little town where she had grown up had begun to feel small and constrained.

Leo, vibrant, dynamic and larger than life, had shown her the incompleteness of the life she'd been living. The prospect of moving to a different place, to open a new chapter in her life, held a certain appeal.

Boston was supposed to be a beautiful city. She would love it. It would be a fresh start and, if Leo was going to be the spoke in the wheel, then she would have to deal with that spoke and get used to it because it wasn't going away any time soon.

Thankfully, she had a reprieve, because he wouldn't be meeting her personally—and why would he, considering she had already been dispatched from his life in terms of marriage material? But she would have to face him sooner rather than later and, when she did, she wasn't going to go to pieces and start getting sentimental.

She wasn't going to think about women he might have been seeing or would be seeing, and she wasn't going to create entire life stories in her head about what might or might not happen in his life over the next few years when it came to finding a partner.

Boston was in the grip of winter cold when she roused herself to notice that the jet was landing. Snow was falling and there was a determined layer of white everywhere, the sort of settled snow that would be around for the long haul.

She would be met at the airport by his car containing his PA, who was called Donna, and she would visit the house he had sourced for her. Everything would go exactly according to plan. Kaya knew that because everything Leo did went just as he wanted it to. She was under no obligation to like the place he had chosen but, unless it was downright objectionable, then what was the point in being fussy?

It wasn't as though this house represented the start of a wonderful life for her with the guy of her dreams. This would be bricks and mortar and, as long as it did the job, then why worry? In time, she would move to a place she would call her own, once she had found her feet and come to terms with her emotions.

It was freezing.

Head down, she rushed towards the long, black car waiting for her.

He saw a slender, graceful figure layered with so much clothing that it was hard to see her shape, and wearing her woolly hat pulled so low down that Leo, waiting behind privacy glass in his chauffeur-driven four-wheel drive, marvelled that she could see anything at all.

He had come. He'd had to come. He couldn't *not*. She'd been holed up in Vancouver and, with each passing minute, the terror of losing her had got more and more acute. Having confronted the thing he'd never dreamt possible, it now had him in its vice-like grip and refused to let him go.

He'd got the message loud and clear that, released from the bind of having to marry him, she was moving out of his orbit. Her disembodied voice down the end of the line had been remote when they had spoken, and she'd shown next to no interest in the various places he had located for her to rent. There was no longer any need for her to grit her teeth, look on the bright side and channel her energies into making the best of the situation, starting with sex.

He thought about her every second of every minute of every day. He adored this woman and, for the first time in his life, he knew what it felt like to be vulnerable and he didn't resent it. He accepted it.

Could he spend the rest of his life like this, tormented? No way.

She pulled open the door, head still down, and it was a couple of seconds before she realised that Leo was in the car, sprawled in the back seat, leaning against the door.

And then she gasped.

What was he doing here?

She looked away quickly. She hadn't had time to rehearse her reaction. She could feel hectic colour flood into her cheeks and she made a business of fussing with her backpack, buckling herself in and slamming the door behind her.

He looked coolly, impossibly sexy in casual black jeans and a tan cashmere jumper, with what looked like a black, long-sleeved, skin-tight tee-shirt underneath.

'I wasn't expecting you.' Kaya schooled her face into a polite smile but her heart was racing, her pulses were pounding and her mouth was dry.

'I know. I...was the trip okay?'

He hated the polite utterance that left his mouth. He wanted to wrap his arms around her, pull her to him and bury his face in her hair. He was afraid. Afraid of a minefield of exposed feelings lying ahead of him. Afraid of being committed to a course of action that would end up going nowhere. Had his rigidly controlled world begun unravelling when the truth about his past had been revealed? Or had he just been waiting for the right woman to come along and break the spell?

Leo didn't know. He stared at her, wishing that he could read what she was thinking.

'Kaya.'

'You said your PA would be showing me the house.'

They spoke at the same time.

Ensnared by the glittering depths of his dark, dark eyes, Kaya could only stare. But then she blinked and reminded herself that this was the guy who had given her the freedom she had asked for because he had no longer seen the value in marrying her, all things considered. She doubted she would ever be able to do more than speculate on his reasons for changing his mind.

She would pretend to be happy if it killed her, so she forced a smile and made a something and nothing remark about them talking over one another.

'How do you feel about moving to Boston?' he asked, buying time.

'I think it's going to be great,' Kaya said

brightly. 'I mean, I'll be able to carry on working remotely with my clients, and then it'll be exciting getting out there and meeting new people.'

'New people...'

'I suppose I became quite accustomed to small-town living, accustomed to doing the same things all the time with the same people. Course, I plan on returning often to visit my old friends, but it's going to be fantastic expanding my social circle.'

'There's nothing wrong with small-town living.'

'I didn't think that was your thing.'

'It never used to be but times change. I've always been a guy who can adapt.' He inhaled shakily. 'Kaya...this situation between us...'

'We've talked about it enough.'

'There are things I have to say to you.'

'I don't want to hear.'

'And I don't want to say them but I have no choice.' Now he knew what it felt like to look down the side of a precipice, one foot outstretched, hoping to make a safe landing on a wing and a prayer. 'Kaya, the past two weeks have been hell.'

Kaya was utterly thrown by that remark.

'What do you mean? No, I don't want to hear.'

'I know you don't. I know you're where you

want to be but please—let me speak. Being apart from you has been unbearable.' He raked his fingers through his hair and realised he was shaking but he didn't care. 'This is maybe not quite the place for a conversation like this but, Kaya, I can't spend this entire trip pretending that everything is okay when nothing is.'

'I have no idea what you're talking about.'

She looked suspicious, bewildered and guarded and for a few seconds Leo wondered whether he had the guts to finish what he'd started, but almost immediately he knew that he had to.

'I've missed you,' he said roughly.

'No!' Her voice was sharp. 'It's not going to work. I'm not going to make the mistake of falling back into bed with you because the sex is good, only to wake up the next day to realise that, in the bigger scheme of things, sex doesn't matter that much. I'm not climbing on a merry-go-round with you, Leo.'

'Is that what you think happened?'

'Like I said, I don't want to talk about this.' She made to look away but he gently caught her chin with his fingers and she froze.

'Tell me why you think I felt I had to…let you walk away from me. From us…from this thing I want more than anything in the world…'

'Because…' Kaya tilted her head defiantly

'…you realised that, if you don't have love in a relationship, then it's never going to succeed.' She half-closed her eyes and breathed in deeply, taking the plunge. 'Or, more likely, you had me out there and you realised what you knew all along—lust is something that comes and goes. It went, and being stuck in a relationship without even the benefit of sex was just never going to work out. The best thing you could do would be to call it a day before it went any further. I get it. I really do.'

'Do you?'

'You didn't have to meet me here just to tell me that. I wasn't born yesterday, Leo. I know who you are. You told me at the start, and a leopard never changes its spots. You don't do commitment, and you don't do love, except now commitment has been forced onto you. But that doesn't mean anything else has been. You don't have to explain your decision to me.'

'You've got it all wrong,' Leo said urgently.

'Which bit? The commitment bit? The getting bored bit?'

'The *everything* bit. I used to be that man, Kaya—locked away in my ivory tower, disciplined and unavailable—but then you came along. I'm not sure when it happened but that man began to morph into someone else.'

'Leo, please don't do this.'

'What?'

'Tell me lies you think I want to hear.'

'I've never lied to a woman in my life before,' Leo protested, flushing darkly. 'I've always thought that it's much better to tell the truth, even if the truth is inconvenient.'

'Then what are you saying?' Kaya heard the agonised longing in her voice and hated herself for it, for that horrible weakness she'd tried so hard to put to bed.

'I'm saying that I love you, Kaya, and that's why I let you go.'

'You love me? You want me to believe that you suddenly love me?' she said angrily.

'I don't blame you for being sceptical. I never thought it would happen, that I would find myself so deeply in love with a woman that I would relinquish everything to do what was right for her. But that's the guy I am now, and that's why I'm here, throwing caution to the winds. I love you. I knew that in your heart you wanted to find your dream, and marrying me, doing what I wanted, would have stood in the way of that dream. I wasn't going to let that happen and so I let you go. I'm telling you this, Kaya, because I couldn't *not*. It's…bigger than me…and if it had never found a voice, if you had walked away without at least knowing how I felt, I would have lived a life of regret for ever.'

'How can I believe you? How?'

'I would never lie to you and I would never lie about this thing I'm feeling. I adore you, Kaya.'

'You never said…'

'I didn't know. I just knew life was empty without you in it.'

'I wish you'd said.'

'Would you have come flying back into my arms?'

'Yes!' Kaya smiled then laughed, swept away on a wave of happiness that was tentative to start with but then gathered momentum, growing bigger and bigger until all her doubts and unhappiness disappeared under its force. 'I've loved you for so long, but I knew that I couldn't say anything because you'd been so adamant that you weren't interested in all that fairy-tale nonsense.'

She reached for him and stroked his cheek. 'I'm so glad you've told me now, so glad you couldn't wait. I love you, my dearest Leo, and I'm never going to stop.'

Leo had wanted them to be married sooner rather than later. At the time, it had been a case of 'why wait?' but then, sooner rather than later, it had become an urgency to have this woman be his wife, wear his ring on her finger.

He ditched the separate Boston townhouse

and moved into the cottage with her, the very cottage he had found and she had loved. They had seen it and walked around it, holding hands, dreaming of a future, and everything had been right in the world.

Leo still sometimes stopped to think how much he had changed and how unimaginable the joys were of not being a slave to making money, of burying himself in the cold world of finance because it was safe.

Having turned his back on his emotions his whole life, he now succumbed to them with equal single-mindedness, because he could think of nothing else he wanted to be than the guy who devoted himself to the woman he loved.

They were married when Kaya was six months' pregnant. The cottage had gone from walls, rooms and empty spaces to a home filled with things she treasured and, here and there, were memories of Julie Anne—whose place in Leo's life was now a peaceful one. Thoughts were treasured of a mother who had loved him and would have kept him close, had fate not got in the way.

'Spending time in my New York penthouse is going to be a culture shock,' he'd said to her, dropping a kiss on her head that first day when they had declared their love and had strolled around the sprawling cottage. They'd discussed what they would do with some of the rooms, before going outside to inspect the generous wild, luxuriant grounds waiting to be turned into all sorts of things that Kaya had already been excited about: an orchard...somewhere for vegetables...a play area...a pond where wildlife would flourish.

'Why?' Kaya had looked at him and smiled but she'd known. This big, powerful man, once so invincible, was the guy who had fallen in love with her and couldn't bear the thought of them being apart.

And, as he never tired of telling her over the weeks and months to come, he had never had a home before he'd met her. He'd only ever had very, very expensive houses.

It was a quiet wedding, with only a handful of close friends there, including some of Julie Anne's, who had countless stories to tell about her and her legendary generosity. And of course her mother and her stepfather, who had travelled from New Zealand and were staying on for a couple of weeks.

They would go and visit, Kaya promised, just as soon as the baby was born and things had settled a bit.

She knew their ranch couldn't be left for too

long and it was incredible that they were staying for as long as they were.

Life was so full and so busy that the months crept upon them with the stealth of a thief in the night, and suddenly brought them a baby girl. Isabella Julie was born at a little after dawn on a crisp autumn morning. As brown as a berry and with a mop of dark curls, she arrived without fuss and was the apple of Leo's eye.

With every smile and every look, Kaya could see just how much he adored his daughter, and just how much he adored *her*.

The guy who had sworn himself off love had come full circle…and for her? Not a second passed by when she wasn't grateful for the love that had found her, the love that had disobeyed both of their red lines and found a way to settle between them until nothing else in the world mattered.

* * * * *